QUEEN OF SEAS

DRAGONS RISING BOOK THREE

ALISHA KLAPHEKE

To my Uncommon Crew and my Dragon Den
I write for YOU

A scream tore from Vahly's throat only to be drowned in salt water. The sea kynd's grip on her was unrelenting, his fingers digging into her flesh as he pulled her through the water, heading deeper into the ocean.

Why hadn't he just killed her on the shore when he had his spear's edge to her throat? What was his purpose in dragging her into the sea?

Visions of torture flashed through her mind: fingernails ripped from their beds; blood pouring from a busted nose; a slow, burning drowning, the water leaking into her lungs bit by bit, driven by spellwork.

She jerked and flailed but accomplished nothing as the incredibly powerful being swam on, his gaze trained on something in the distance as if he didn't even notice her struggling. The water stung Vahly's eyes; Arc's eyewort and magic were disappearing. Her heart slammed against her chest.

When would she be unable to breathe? How deep

would they be when her human body, not made like a sea kynd's, would crumple beneath the pressure? Surely any second the magic would fail, then whatever torture this male had in mind would be pointless because she'd be dead.

She closed her eyes against the water and tried to feel the earth's power inside her chest, humming, drumming, singing in her veins. But the pulse was weak and she couldn't smell anything at all, let alone turned earth, trees, or verdant mosses.

The sea kynd pulled Vahly onto a black coral shelf, then into a forest of slick kelp that clung to her body. He pushed her down and put a foot on her throat. The coral bit into her back as she grabbed one of his webbed toes and yanked with all she had. His foot slipped only a fraction before he had her again, pinned like one of the dead butterflies in the study boxes at the Lapis library. The coral shredded her vest and cut through to her flesh, but pain didn't come. Blood stampeded through her veins and adrenaline made her numb.

"Stop struggling. There is no use." The sea kynd's voice thundered through the water, roaring with the magic that allowed his kynd to speak so clearly under the water.

The desperate urge to demand answers, to ask why he was keeping her alive, tore at Vahly's throat, but she knew her voice had no such magic. If she opened her mouth to speak, the words would only be garbled nonsense and the water might decide to rush into her lungs and finish the job before her captor had the pleasure of doing it himself.

His gaze, eyes wide and irises too black, darted over her face as he studied her. Water lifted his dark hair and the ends of his beard above his bare chest. He wore loose blue-black trousers that were tightly affixed at the ankles. Foamy bubbles crowded around his coral spear like magic just itching to strike out at her.

He lowered the spear, whispered three words, then pointed the weapon at Vahly.

Her heart hung for a beat, dead in her chest.

Power pushed the water over her face and chest and throat like one thousand hands pressing and pushing and scraping. Then the magic slithered over her body to her legs. An invisible weight clamped onto her lower half. A searing pain lashed across the sides of her neck. Her fingers flew up to feel the damage his spellwork had wrought.

Tiny flaps of skin undulated beneath her fingertips.

She shuddered.

Gills.

She had gills.

The magic shivered away, leaving only a tingling in her throat and a heaviness in her limbs.

"Speak," the sea kynd demanded. He used the tongue of the dragons. But of course, Vahly's mind distantly reminded her, sea kynd knew all the tongues spoken. They used their knowledge to name threats they saw to their world, to make declarations of war and blood.

A cough erupted from Vahly's throat, and he removed his foot, allowing her to float to a standing position. She was definitely heavier, or she would've drifted to the surface. So this was how the sea folk walked along the bottom of the ocean. Vahly's stomach rolled at the feeling, and she clutched her middle, afraid she was about to retch.

She fought the anxiety and nausea, then managed to straighten and face him.

"Did you—" Another cough tore through her. "Did you turn me into a sea kynd?"

Images of her gryphon familiar, Kyril, as well as Nix, Arc, and Amona washed across her heart, stinging, lashing, burning. If she were changed, she'd never see them again. She'd be on the wrong side of the world, the war. Cut away from them. A sob caught in her throat and she squeezed her eyes shut, unable to cry, of course, because now she was one of them, a creature unable to properly weep, to feel, to empathize. Vahly felt as though she were being stretched apart, like the agony of losing everyone too soon without having the chance to properly fight for their lives would rip her into pieces as surely as any sea kynd's teeth.

But at that moment, the sea kynd stared down at her, his lips parted. His teeth weren't jagged, sharp maybe, but more like her own teeth and Arc's. For some reason, her fear settled into the back of her mind. Shock, that was it, she thought distantly. This was her mind's defense against this horror.

"You don't have razor teeth," she said in a warbled, stunned voice.

He cocked his head and glared, fury and confusion warring in his features. His frighteningly black eyes blinked as he studied her face. He opened his mouth as if he were about to say something, but then closed it again.

Her senses drowning, overwhelmed, Vahly snapped, "If you're going to kill me, why not just do it?" Her throat was on fire, and her words punched through the water. It had to be an effect of the magic he'd performed on her.

The sea kynd's mouth twisted into a grimace. He yanked Vahly's ivory-handled sword from her belt and thrust it into the water. The sword had been a prized gift from her mother, and a piece of Vahly sank with the weapon that was as familiar to her as her own hand. The words Amona had spoken the day she'd given the sword rushed through Vahly's mind. *Fight the sea with the sea,* Amona had said, speaking of the sea creature's tusk that had been fashioned into a hilt. Well, Vahly wouldn't be doing that, it seemed. Her shoulders sagged, body weak with despair.

Raising his coral spear, the sea kynd glared. His eyes held her death.

She'd done it. He had been showing mercy, and she'd agitated him enough to make him finish this job.

CHAPTER TWO

Ryton looked away, his mind spinning with memories of Selene, of the blood that stained the water. "I don't know why I haven't ended you yet. You deserve to die for helping the monsters slaughter my family."

The Earth Queen laughed, a sickly sound. "Oh, and you haven't killed scores of theirs?"

He jerked her up, staring her in the face. Her flesh was slimy under his fingers, her body's weakness incongruent with the fear that Queen Astraea had shown at the mere mention of this Earth Queen's name.

He studied her pale, eerie eyes. The scent of her turned his stomach. "We have only killed because we must."

"Just like you *must* drown the entire world in salt water?"

He twisted to take in fresh salt water, to rid his body of the taste of trees and dirt that oozed from the human like a plague. "If we don't, the dragons will continue to wipe our species out."

"And what about the elves? They haven't done anything to you in ages. Your queen will annihilate them too in this grand plan of hers."

He refused to listen to anything that came out of her mouth. He set his spear's edge beneath the line of her jaw. "The elves are aiding you and the dragons as well. They aren't innocents. They're disgusting creatures with no respect for—"

"And just how many elves have you befriended?"

"I have known their spies." He shuddered.

"The worst of the elves. Surely you have to realize that a spy is not a proper representation of a species."

His knuckles whitened around his spear. She was weaving the situation to fit her own version of the truth, and he was finished listening to her, his enemy, friend to those who had taken sweet Selene and so many others. Their screams echoed in his head.

Blood pounding through his veins, he lifted his spear, then brought the flat edge down, hitting the Earth Queen sharply across the head. Her body went limp, unconscious.

Taking her by the hair, he swam toward Tidehame, toward Queen Astraea and his kynd. The memory of Selene had stayed his hand, kept him from killing this human, but it was up to Astraea to decide the Earth Queen's final fate.

Was he a coward in this? Most likely.

Perhaps he would kill her before they reached Tidehame and it would all be over. Maybe he would torture her for information about numbers of dragons and their locations. Either way, he needed a place to keep her prisoner, a spot that could hold her and possibly further dampen her magical abilities.

A place in the deepest part of the ocean.
He knew just the spot. Scar Chasm.

CHAPTER THREE

Nix spread her wings over the glittering sea, her body dangerously close to water that might still hold the sea kynd assassin.

Vahly! she shouted through her mind, hoping the telepathy gained from Vahly's bond with Kyril would still work. *Are you alive? Please answer us. Arc will come for you. I will get backup from Queen Cassiopeia. Keep fighting, my girl!*

A surge of desperation threatened to drop Nix right out of the air. If she lost Vahly, she'd have lost so much more than a savior for the world. She'd lose her dearest, darling friend. Her wings shuddered as she veered toward the coast.

Kyril flew circles above the spot where Vahly had last been seen, where the sea kynd had grabbed her and pulled her into the waves. He keened, the feathers and fur on his neck and head puffed to make him appear larger. He was roughly the size of Amona, so the sight of his claws extended and his fierce eagle eyes made even Nix feel a stab of fear. The gryphon's head turned this way and that as he searched the white-tipped expanse for Vahly's golden head.

It burned Nix's already shattered heart.

Arc stood not far from Kyril's circling shadow. Bared to the waist and bootless, the elf was weaving a powerful spell for himself. The magic—spinning tendrils of dark purple and pinpoints of brightness—would supposedly keep him well and hale for an extended period under the sea.

Nix landed beside Arc, shaking her head, her eyes threatening to give way to tears. She didn't want to waste time transforming so she spoke to him telepathically.

Can you hear me, Arcturus?

He lifted his chin, magic churning like spilled paint around his fingers. Arcturus' slightly canted, elven eyes held a world of sorrow, bloodshot through and over-bright. Every moment Vahly was missing was another step closer to his death. She knew well what grief could do, how it scraped the soul bare, and Arcturus wouldn't handle it well. Despite his age and the mysterious and dangerous edge to him, he was one of those eternal innocents, heart laid plain for the lashing. Poor fellow.

I can hear you, he said. *No sign of her?*

Nix's throat clenched and she took a shaky breath, Kyril's cries ripping at her chest. *None. And she didn't answer me. I'm off to find Cassiopeia and secure you some non-dragon, salt-water-proof backup. Can they all weave a spell like yours and somehow find you down there?*

The thought of venturing into the black pit of death that was the ocean had Nix shivering.

Not all of them will be able to cast this spell. But Cassiopeia will and the Council members as well. Those who cannot can be protected by those who are able. My kynd know where Tidehame is, and I can only assume the sea kynd male will bring Vahly there, to see Queen Astraea, so we will head that way.

Arc's magic peeled away from his hands and shimmered into his body, dissolving and disappearing. He stepped forward and put a hand on Nix's snout. She tipped her head and nudged his chest, wishing she could help him bear this more easily, but she was too overcome herself and didn't have much more to give. Hopelessness was like night approaching, darkening her sight of what they had to do, what they must at least attempt.

Kyril landed clumsily beside them, then crowded into the warmth of their little circle, his body so much larger than the two of theirs. He lifted his beak and shrieked into the cloud-swept sky, and Nix finally lost her hold and wept openly. Arc's trembling hand slid to her shoulder, and through tears, Nix could see Arc's other hand pressed to Kyril's chest. The gryphon bowed his head, beak touching Arc's shoulder.

Please take him with you, Arc said. *He must be kept busy.*

Kyril flashed an image of Vahly's face as she'd been captured. His liquid eyes found Nix's.

We will find an army for our girl, Kyril. Perk up. We have hope still! Nix forced life into her words even though they felt foolish and sad and far too small.

I must go, Arc said, breaking away and walking toward the rocky shore. He raised a hand. *Once I free Vahly, we will meet you at the Lost Valley. May the wind carry you quickly!*

With that, he leapt from the coast in a wide arc, turning once in the air before diving into the broken blue of the sea.

Nix extended her wings, took a few steps, then lifted

from the ground, amazed she could manage flight as heavy as her heart sat in her chest.

Kyril squawked, then sprang upward, soaring into the sky, his gray-blue wings like a storm following in Nix's wake.

Surely the elves would be quick to join Arc. Their magic was Vahly's only chance at escaping her watery grave.

CHAPTER FOUR

V ahly woke to a headache that could've broken the world. She blinked, vision blurry, only to remember where she was.

In the ocean.

Her scalp was numb, and her feet were missing their boots. Confused, she reached up. And felt large, finned fingers twined roughly into her hair.

Everything came rushing back.

Heart hammering, she touched her new gills, then struggled against the sea kynd, who held her by the hair, kicking and twisting and scratching at his flesh. He didn't seem to notice, and her nails took little away for their work. His skin was thick and rough, impervious to any damage she might try to inflict. Finally, she took hold of his hand with both of hers, kicked hard through the water, and jerked him off course. He spun, yanking her hair and pulling her face to see his.

"If you won't come quietly, I'll simply have to render

you less troublesome." Wearing a flat look, he whipped his spear through the water, across her thigh.

Pain burst over her skin, and blood curled from a deep cut.

"You could die from this. But if I get you to where we're going, we can heal you. Now, stop struggling or you'll only speed your death and ruin your one chance to live." He took off again, twice as fast this time, his grip now on her upper arm.

Stomach rolling, Vahly screamed a frustrated shout into the foggy expanse of waving seaweed and sparkling schools of fish. "Why heal me when you want me dead?"

"It is the queen's choice now."

He was an idiot. A scary idiot, but one just the same. "You make no sense, sea fool." Her leg throbbed in rhythm with her pulse.

They swam over an empty stretch of sand that twisted up and into the water in great columns. A sleek fish the size of her captor darted toward Vahly, then swam abruptly away only to circle back again. Vahly's nerves were raw, overworked, incapable of further horror, but she knew this thing was out for a meal. It had the same twitching excitement she'd seen in younger dragons before a kill.

"You have competition, sea kynd," she murmured, the world fading then clearing. "I think this one wants to rule my future. In his mouth."

The sea kynd whirled and threw his spear. The bright color sped like lightning through the water and pierced the large fish through the side. Blood cascaded from the dying, falling fish as the spear flipped and soared back to the sea kynd's outstretched hand.

"Ah. So that's how you do it. I've always wondered." Vahly's words slurred as she drifted into unconsciousness.

RYTON GRITTED HIS TEETH, THINKING OF HOW THIS CREATURE had fought side by side with dragons and now he'd given her information. Why hadn't he just killed her? She was right. He was a fool.

The blood from her wounded leg was a banner marking their progress northward. Unless she was very strong indeed, she would die from this wound, and he'd be spared the duty to kill a being his sister would've found so interesting, one he himself was curious about, even if he'd never admit it.

The outskirts of Tidehame appeared in the distance, a rock wall covered in pearly shells and undulating seaweed that marked the civilization's boundary. Ryton took the Earth Queen the long way around the border and headed for the far end of Scar Chasm, where not even the most daring of the nautili harvesters and rare fish seekers swam.

The ocean floor dropped steadily, fifty feet below, then one hundred, before it showed the deep line of darkness in the bedrock. Ryton rushed into the Chasm. The walls rose to either side, and fish with glowing eyes flashed past. Cold as a corpse, the water here touched Ryton unlike a chill usually did. And it tasted off, too metallic. The liquid was slick in his mouth and along his sensitive fins. Once the Chasm swallowed them, in a place where even Ryton could barely see, he set the human against the western wall. With a length of braided salt-twine, he bound each of her hands to a branch of petrified coral behind her, then set to work healing her leg.

Because he had clearly lost his mind.

Hating himself, painfully confused, he spoke the healing spell, whispering into the sudden bubbling of water and the roar of magic in his ears.

The Earth Queen's eyes fluttered open. She looked down, but she only frowned. "Did you heal me? I can't see, but..." Her head lolled to one side, and she blinked, obviously trying to wake from the stupor of blood loss. "Fool. Do me a final favor and just kill me. I'll never make it out of here."

She flexed her fingers as if she could work a spell. The ocean suffocated her power, but she was quick, so he kept his focus on her. She'd used the earthen objects in the sunken ruins of Bihotzetik to fight him and might have abilities he couldn't comprehend. Her talk was only meant to lull him into a false sense of security.

"Don't play games with me."

"But I love games," she mumbled, her words still weak and running together. "Did you know I'm a fantastic gambler? No? Well, I'm betting on you this time, sea kynd."

Ryton's jaw ached, and his muscles twitched with tension. He longed to kill this beast. But he just...couldn't. "If you die, your elf and your dragons die. Why would you goad me into slaying you before you've had a chance to escape?"

Her eyes squeezed shut, and her stomach tensed beneath her ripped clothing like she was in great pain. "Maybe not. Elves are a wily sort."

"And why are we talking about the race I recently

obliterated?" Astraea swam out of the darkness, four guards flanking her.

The human let out a small moan at Astraea's announcement. "Arcturus," she mumbled, head dropping and chest heaving.

Ryton went very still, his jaw tight. He should've gone straight to Astraea. "My queen." He bowed, his heart punctuating his every word with a loud thump. How had she—his queen, his lover, his torturous addiction—found him here?

But Astraea only stared at the human, ignoring Ryton. She swam lazily, gaze locked on her nemesis, finally face to face.

To her merit, the Earth Queen didn't look shaken. In fact, she'd gained some color in her cheeks and she managed to return Astraea's glare in full force.

"So you're the piece of work we're all trying to deal with these days," the Earth Queen said as she cocked her head and looked Astraea up and down. The human lifted her eyebrows and pursed her lips like she wasn't impressed, but her shaking body told a different tale.

Astraea grinned, pearly teeth flashing in the dark. "I suppose I am. I'm so glad you've heard good things." She swam closer and placed a finger above the human's heart.

Ryton held his breath. This was it. Astraea would end this Earth Queen, and then they would flood the land, and eventually, his kynd would find peace.

But instead of delivering the killing blow, Astraea turned to Ryton, her finger still on the human's chest.

"Ryton, darling. Why in all the waves did you decide to

waste your time and mine by torturing this abomination and not simply offing her immediately?"

"That's what I asked him," the Earth Queen said, wearing an insanely cocky grin. She had definitely lost too much blood.

Astraea flicked the human's new gills with a sharp fingernail. The Earth Queen flinched, swallowing convulsively. "And," Astraea continued, "you've turned her into a sick mimic of one of us. I can't say that I like this play, General Ryton."

Ryton swallowed, his throat dry and his tongue bitter-tasting. "Forgive me, my queen, but you too are holding back, or the creature would already be dead."

Astraea laughed, the sound bouncing off Scar Chasm's walls and sending bubbles rushing toward the surface. She eyed her guards. "You see? This is why he is my favorite. Never dull, this one! So full of spice."

Ryton exhaled, his body sagging with shameful relief. He should've been glad to die for his kynd, for this foolish move he'd made in preserving the Earth Queen with a spell that twisted what it meant to be sea kynd.

CHAPTER FIVE

Vahly's strength was coming back to her, but she almost wished she'd simply faded away. "The elves. You killed them all." It wasn't a question. Queen Astraea had stated the fact, but Vahly hoped to get more information from her. How? When?

"Their queen died before my eyes." Astraea blinked, tiny bubbles like jewels on her blue-green eyelashes. The Sea Queen's eerie beauty unsettled Vahly. "It was exciting," Astraea said. "She fought hard, and I respect her for that. She died defending some of her own. But the elves had to be eliminated because they aided you, little Earth Queen."

Vahly's bravado slipped as the weight of so many deaths pulled her heart into an abyss. Cassiopeia. All of her kynd. Gone. Vahly was tied to the rock wall, but she felt as though she sank, deeper and deeper into an impossible darkness.

And Arc. The pain he would feel when he found out…

Nausea swelled through Vahly, making her gag. Arc, Nix, and Kyril would go there, to the Forest of Illumahrah, and they would find nothing but corpses and destruction, a muddy mass grave.

Fire sparked through Vahly's blood. She couldn't let grief overtake her. She had to keep trying because she knew her friends would never give up.

While this Ryton and his horrifying queen discussed how a patrol had seen Ryton swimming with Vahly and reported back, Vahly pressed her wrists against the jagged coral and rubbed her bindings, trying to get them to break.

"Oh, yes," Astraea was saying, "our kynd was rather fascinated when they heard you had captured a human who could somehow survive in our world. They knew who she had to be. And of course, I too was breathless to meet this adversary, the one we never thought would rise." She grinned at Vahly with blood-red lips. "I do so enjoy a good fight."

She didn't look like a warrior. The Sea Queen wore a scarlet crown of coral inlaid with pearls and based in gold. Her dress seemed ill-suited to a battle, all flimsy and pearl-strewn. No, Astraea wasn't like any warrior Vahly had ever seen, but there was no doubt that this queen was deadly, and that was what scared Vahly the most. The strangeness of it, the question of how such a creature would attack, the confusion of smiles mixed with vicious bloodlust. The Sea Queen's teeth looked much like Ryton's, not razor-edged like the dragons' stories claimed. But that didn't mean she couldn't bite as well as any meat-eating beast.

Astraea probably ate hearts for breakfast.

The coral wasn't slicing through Vahly's bindings as well as she'd hoped. Since her bound wrists were hidden well behind her, she rubbed harder, the branch cutting into her wrists beside her numb palms. Flexing her fingers to get the blood back into them, she kept her gaze on the sea kynd and tried not to draw attention to her efforts.

The first binding snapped, and her left hand was free. She gripped the coral branch, pretending she remained trapped, and while she worked on the other, she attempted to feel the Earth's heartbeat inside the rock wall at her back. There was some sort of drumming, but the rhythm was different here. This stone wall had been born to the sea, and it would refuse her command. Maybe if she could get down to the bedrock…

"Take her," Astraea said, gesturing to Vahly. "We will question her in a nicer spot, General. Although I do appreciate your penchant for drama." She set a hand against Ryton's chest and another lower on his abdomen.

Vahly raised an eyebrow. They were lovers. That might be something Vahly could use, an angle to work. If she lived long enough to create a plan.

Her second binding snapped as the guards—one fair and the other barrel-chested–swam forward. She would lose this, but why not bloody a nose or two?

When the light-skinned guard was within reach, Vahly slammed her palm into the sea kynd's face. He jerked, gargling in a flurry of bubbles as blood clouded around his white hair. The second guard lurched toward her, an arm up to block his face. Vahly grabbed his groin area and twisted his short trousers hard. His shout of pain rippled the water.

"Enough." Astraea raised her spear and spoke two words, and the world around Vahly went black.

CHAPTER SIX

Astraea led the group out of Scar Chasm's black waters and into the main current that pulled them easily along toward the center of Tidehame and the palace. So the secret was out. The Earth Queen had risen, and they had her in hand. Now what...

She had to act as though this was her plan all along and retain the illusion that she had everything completely under control and the flood's success was now secure. This was a chance to flaunt her power over this fiend who'd sided with the loathsome dragons.

Astraea smiled. Yes. That was it. She would parade this Earth Queen through the streets, beaten and broken, crushed beneath the might of Astraea's reign, her power, her cunning.

Folk were already filtering out of their homes and shops along the main route through Tidehame. They whispered and pointed at Astraea and her captive. Light spilled from more doorways and windows as young and old, rich and poor emerged to witness the spectacle.

Spinning, Astraea addressed Ryton and the others. "Bind the human's wrists to your spear, General."

Ryton did as he was told, and the Earth Queen's eyes opened as he worked. The Earth Queen's face gave away no emotion, but Astraea could smell her fear in the water.

Once the little queen was secured to the spear that rested across her bony shoulders, Astraea called up a current. Churning water lifted the enemy queen and pushed her slowly down the street to the sounds of the crowd's abuse.

"Yes!" Astraea smiled down at her subjects. "I have delivered the Earth Queen to you." She cackled, enjoying using the powerful title for one brought so low. "I know some of you were worried about the threat of this one's rise to power," she said, glancing at the guild council's gray-and-blue-bearded host beside the gathering house's immense, pale columns. "The human, the last chance of the vicious and vile land creatures, is humbled and stripped of her strength. She will die at my own hand after I extract from her valuable information about our greatest enemies, the dragons."

A young man not yet bearded stepped forward, fist raised at the Earth Queen. "Dragon lover!" He spoke a weak spell, then threw a rotted starfish. His mother, mouth drawn with fear, pulled him back as the starfish hit the human's cheek and slithered down her body, leaving a trail of foul-smelling muck.

This was exactly what they needed. A nice boost to their morale at the hands of their Sea Queen.

Astraea lifted her own spear, smiling. "Wonderful! No, don't hold him back. Do as you see fit to this abomination, my kynd. Show her how you feel about her one true desire, the desire to thrust a foul steel sword through your hearts and the hearts of your loved ones!"

The crowd began shouting and hurling spoiled fish at the human. Astraea swam higher to avoid the mess, her soul brimming with joy at the sight of a particularly large sea apple striking the Earth Queen directly in the throat. The human coughed and tried to double over as another rotten apple hit her stomach with the force of someone who was quite good at thrusting spells. But the Earth Queen couldn't double over. Astraea's spelled salt water kept her body upright and moving steadily down the thoroughfare.

Ryton's lip curled as he watched the show. Good. He was just as disgusted with the human as Astraea was. She had wondered for a brief moment just why he hadn't killed her. The creature did have a youthful softness to her still, a characteristic that some might find deserving of mercy. Of course, Ryton wouldn't be swayed by such nonsense. He was Astraea's dearest friend and the shining example of what a military leader could achieve.

The palace came into view, comforting in its splendor and familiarity.

Sagging, the human groaned. Bruises purpled the flesh that showed past her sleeves and along her neck and collarbone.

Astraea had the urge to close the distance between them and break every one of her fingers, relishing the snap of her arrogant bones. How dare she think she could fight the Sea Queen. But there would be time enough for revenge.

CHAPTER SEVEN

"Take her to the tower," Astraea said to the guards before turning to Ryton. "And you will come with me, General. I would love to hear about the fine work you've done." She eyed the glistening creature that rode across his upper back. Its legs were like jointed spears, and power hummed from its body, rippling the water in lines that surrounded Ryton's head like a halo fish's flamboyant fins. "I need to know all about the magnificent magic you gained along your journey."

Two of Astraea's strongest, swiftest guards—one ginger-headed and the other a head taller than Ryton—took up the limp Earth Queen and swam her toward the back of the palace where the tower rose from the sea bed.

Surprisingly, Ryton shuddered as he glanced at his shoulder at one of the creature's legs. "Yes, of course, my queen. Will General Grystark attend our meeting?"

Before Astraea could craft a lie, one of the remaining guards opened his stupid mouth.

"Oh, General Ryton, General Grystark is no longer with us."

Astraea bit back a snarl, linked her arm in Ryton's, and hurried them through the gates and into the corridor that led to her chambers.

"Did you send General Grystark on a mission?"

"We have been busy since you left. Using your genius tunnel, we attacked the elven homeland."

Ryton pulled to a stop, his eyes flashing. "I didn't realize... And it worked? The tunnel allowed safe passage under the entire island?"

She forgave him for not using her title. He was excited and deserved mercy. "Indeed. We had to rid the world of those foul beasts. They were aiding our enemies and had in truth become enemies too. All is well now."

Two guards opened her chamber doors, and as Astraea and Ryton entered, Astraea left Ryton's side to rest her tired legs. The singer she'd taken in—Larisa—bowed deeply as Astraea sprawled on her couch and rubbed the fatigue from the fins along her ankles.

"Sing something for us," Astraea said. "An old song, one of the early Sea Queen ballads."

Larisa's voice rose to a ringing, mellow note before tumbling down, her words bringing the golden age of the sea to mind.

"...on glittering currents,
Deep lengths to explore,
Gold and pearl and marble halls,
Dancers in the coral court..."

Ryton hovered in the center of the room, the nautili and

seaweed casting golden light over his shoulders and forehead. He looked confused at Larisa's presence.

"My queen. So you weren't simply baiting the human about the elves' demise? The elven alchemist who traveled with her lives still. I saw him with my own eyes. Unfortunately, I wasn't able to slay her cohorts."

That elf would die the moment he was within reach. "Who else was present when you abducted her?" Astraea asked. "Tell me everything."

Astraea half listened as he detailed his visit with the Watcher, how she'd set that magical beast upon his back to enable his body to live out of the water, about the gryphon familiar the Earth Queen had bonded to her, and the dragons who aided her consistently.

Astraea's mind was on Grystark's wife, Lilia. She should have had the female killed so she didn't race to Ryton to tell him of Grystark's death, but Lilia was sly and difficult to nail down. To make matters worse, in a display of how shallow her loyalty to her kynd was, she grieved furiously instead of showing the proper pride in her husband's sacrifice. And now, Lilia had completely disappeared. Astraea could have had her hunted down, but honestly, she wasn't worth the trouble as long as she stayed away and didn't rile Ryton up about the loss.

Astraea would tell him in time. At the right moment. He would understand. After all, Ryton had given up the simple life he loved so much and taken on that magic beast to save the sea kynd and ensure Astraea's success. He was truly loyal. It would be fine. He would understand Grystark's sacrifice.

Unless perhaps he heard the story from a soft-hearted

warrior who'd witnessed the events and the way Grystark had fought Astraea's order to move forward in the face of the tunnel's probable danger.

The loss had been well worth the cost. The plague was no more, and her kynd mated and gave birth every day now. Plus, with the new magic of multiplying water, they had no need for massive armies to fight the dragons.

Astraea rose from her couch and went to Ryton, who was collecting a net of tideberries for her. She ran a fingertip along the shiny shell of the beast clamped onto his back. The thing's power snapped against her finger like a small lightning bolt.

"Will you always wear this, then, able to crawl out of the sea?"

She hoped there was a limit to the time he was permitted to use the creature, for its presence obviously drained him. Gray circles marred his fine eyes, and his cheeks had sunken. Of course, the ability to give chase to land kynd was a power indeed, but it would be of little use once they flooded the land.

Her finger strayed to Ryton's jawline as she circled him, then she looked into his face, the features she knew as well as her own. He was the only one she trusted. Taking the net of tideberries from his hand, she set it aside on a blue coral hook by the mother-of-pearl cabinets. His lips parted.

"Kiss me, Ryton, and let's forget our work for just a little while. I've been so anxious with you gone."

Confusion flickered over his features, and she understood. Normally, she'd never admit to any weakness, but by showing a bit of vulnerability, she would draw him closer to her. He would feel the urge to care for her, and his sense of loyalty would keep this mighty general firmly on her side of any argument.

She didn't wait for him to question her; she kicked away from the sand-strewn, mosaic floor and pressed her body against his. Her breasts heaved as she breathed in his scent, stone and salty magic, and then he kissed her of his own accord.

His lips were full and strong and she wanted to devour them, to force them to submit under light sweeps of her mouth and small bites with her sharp teeth. Despite the drain of the magical beast on his back, his arms tightened around her and he returned her vicious embrace with more fervor than she'd seen from him in ages.

She pulled back, her heart light. "Ryton," she said breathlessly. "Has your heart grown fonder of your queen due to your dangerous mission?"

His throat moved in a disjointed swallow. His cheeks were flushed. "I believe so. I had doubts, my queen, about our goal. But now, here with you…" He took her face in his large hands, the soft webbing between his fingers brushing her ears. "This is where I'm meant to be, with my kynd, serving my queen. I am sorry that I wavered."

Astraea wrapped her arms around his neck, feeling the creature's questioning pinchers and possibly its mouth. She didn't fear it. In fact, she could feel its trepidation at her power, a vibration through the twisting water. It drew its pinchers away as she tightened her grip on Ryton, pulling his mouth to her neck.

With wild abandon, he kissed her from ear to shoulder, his mouth rough. He whispered apologies and affirmations of his dedication to her and to their goal of flooding the foul land beasts so all sea kynd could be safe.

"...no matter what Selene would say of it," he mumbled, still kissing her shoulder. "I cannot bend to fit what her youthful, ignorant heart saw for this world and I—"

Something scratched at Astraea's glad mood. She gently pushed away even though his attention was pleasurable. "Selene?"

Ryton's eyes were wide. He looked mad. "My sister. The one the dragons burned alive during her first mission."

Astraea took a deep breath through her gills, the water smooth and cool along her throat and around her mouth and nose. "Ah. Of course. Did your sister have something to do with you not immediately killing the Earth Queen? Was that your true reason?"

Ryton looked past her to the windows beyond the balcony. "I admit it, my queen. Yes. Selene was always very curious, and my hand couldn't move against the human when Selene's memory rose so clearly. She would've wanted to study the human, to appreciate the differences. She had been interested in the other kynd and how they lived."

Stepping back and crossing her arms, Astraea studied Ryton's open look, the flash of memories in his dark eyes. "A dangerous interest," she said.

"She was young."

"Indeed."

"But I know what we must do. The Earth Queen must die."

"And she must die well."

Ryton cocked his head, not picking up Astraea's line of thinking.

"You see, dear general," she said, swimming around him and smoothing a hand along his lower back, "we will torture her for information and make her presence here useful. Then, we will present her to the Lapis right as we raise the waves that will end them forever."

"Present her?"

Astraea licked her lips. This was rather enjoyable, having Ryton so interested and all her plans finally coming to fruition. "Oh, yes. I believe a cage of scarlet coral that matches my crown would be quite poetic, don't you? We'll keep her alive. Barely. And let her say goodbye to her beloved Lapis matriarch." Astraea hissed and gripped her spear. She threw the weapon into a grassy target on the far wall, making Larisa jump. "I have your pet, Amona," Astraea whispered. "And her suffering will be the last thing you see."

CHAPTER EIGHT

Vahly's eyes opened to a hazy world of deep blue and green. Her throat convulsed, and her hand went to her neck, feeling gills.

"Right," she croaked out, fighting the sickness of fear and grief with sharp-edged humor. "I've become my enemy. Waking nightmare, check."

The sea kynd had tied her to a stone shelf where her changed body with its thick skin and heaviness rested as if she were on land without the shift and lift of water all around. Her boots were gone, and she moved her toes, sickened by the webbing that spanned between them.

Panic rose like a scream around Vahly's pounding heart. Her soul longed for Kyril's warmth, Arc's strength, and Nix's smile. The earth magic inside Vahly pined for the Lost Valley, pushing at her with a power weakened by the sea but insistent nonetheless.

What was Kyril thinking right now?

That she was gone for good?

She imagined him keening and circling the coastline, refusing to rest, falling into the churning tides…

Vahly's chest shook and she gritted her teeth, forcing herself to remain calm. Shrieking and thrashing wouldn't fix this. She had to use what a life of cons and thievery had taught her and create a plan. Fisting her grimy—and now webbed—fingers, she focused on moving forward instead of allowing the situation to drown her, both figuratively and literally.

Her magic tugged at her middle, urging her, pleading with her to leave at once for the Lost Valley, for the place of her birth. She had to stand with Kyril there and recite something. A spell perhaps. Or an oath. The words flitted through her thoughts like nearly transparent moths. She had to get out of here. Now.

Three walls made of the same sooty rock of her bed-like shelf rose closely around her. A row of tightly bunched, black coral created the fourth wall, and a door had been set into the center, complete with what looked like a lock. The floor didn't provide any errant sticks or slim metal pieces to pick said lock. It was only sand and—

Vahly jerked against her bindings. That was it. Sand might mean she was at the bottom of the sea. Maybe if she planted her palms against the bedrock, beneath the sand, her magic would answer her call. As she'd done earlier, she scraped her wrist bindings against the rock, trying to cut herself free. But this time, the stuff they'd used as ties was rubbery, and the rock didn't affect it.

How much water was above her head? Miles of it? How many miles?

She held her breath. How was she ever going to escape?

And what was happening with Arc, Kyril, and Nix? Had they been attacked? Did they think she was dead?

Stop it, she told herself. Stop it right now. Focus.

The stone wasn't going to cut the bindings, but maybe her new claw-like nails could.

Curling her hands so that her middle two fingers brushed the rubbery material that gripped her wrists, she dug with her nails. Pain flared where the nails scratched her skin, but this new flesh didn't break as easily. Hands spasming with the strain on her muscles and tendons, she managed to clip the outer edge of one tie. Finally, she had to relax her hands. It was too much. And all she'd accomplished was a tiny cut in one of her four bindings.

Time to try another tactic.

Lifting up as best she could, bound as she was, she strained to see if anyone was outside her cell guarding her. But all was dim and quiet, aside from the constant shush of water in her ears and the insistent drum of her heart.

Maybe if she faked some sort of incident, someone would come. At least then she'd have more options.

"Guards! I can't breathe! If I die, the queen won't be able to question me!" She coughed violently. That part was incredibly easy to fake because her transformation still felt so wrong.

A male sea kynd wearing the same uniform as her captor, Ryton, swam up to the coral bars. He wore loose trousers—fitted above the ankle to allow use of the fin that ran along the back of the ankle and heel—and had a bare chest. He too had a coral spear, although his was far shorter. Water foamed around the weapon's tip, magic hissing and ready. The sea kynd cocked his head of bright orange hair and studied Vahly.

She coughed again before going limp like she'd slipped into unconsciousness.

It worked.

Through one slitted eye, Vahly watched him touch his spear to the lock. The door sprang open, and he rushed to her side. He pressed a hand to her gills and then set his palm on her chest, just below her throat. His chilly touch sent unpleasant shivers down Vahly's torso. He whispered four words in the sea kynd tongue, and Vahly's body rose an inch from its resting spot. Her eyes flew open as energy surged through her veins.

The sea kynd raised his ginger eyebrows as if in question.

Now was the moment. She had to think of some way to get out of these bindings so she could access the bedrock.

Giving the male doe eyes, Vahly thanked him. "Could I please just sit up?" Hopefully, he understood the language of dragons. Ryton and Astraea had used it in front of her for part of their conversation, so perhaps they all knew it. "I think I'll have trouble again if I am forced to lie flat."

The guard glanced to the open door, then back. "The queen will be here very soon. Do not try to escape. You will only suffer more for disobedience. Our queen does not show mercy to enemies."

Vahly nodded, trying to look weak even though she actually felt strong.

The guard untied her ankles, then one wrist, helping her to sit on the rock shelf. Vahly gave him a smile of thanks as he walked directly to the door and locked it. As soon as he was out of sight, she stretched a foot to touch the sandy ground. Tugging at the tie that held her wrist on the shelf nearly up against the wall, she pushed the grit aside, toes searching for hard earth.

A smooth surface cooled the ball of her foot. She'd reached it.

But her magic didn't rise, drumming and echoing with power like it normally did when she touched the earth with bare flesh or personal weapon. She squeezed her eyes shut, concentrating, trying to feel the earth, the magic, the power.

Nothing.

Squinting toward the ground, she saw glittering pieces of white stone, gold, and pale green shells. She scattered more of the sand. It was an old mosaic floor, worn and patchy in places. Maybe this cell was a part of an older palace or domicile. Regardless, she wouldn't be touching any bedrock here.

She blew out a frustrated breath, forgetting for a moment that she was underwater. The gust came out in waves of sound and force, her gills vibrating and tickling her neck. She was a sea kynd now. Hopefully, not forever. Stones and Blackwater, please, not forever.

A thought occurred to her. She straightened.

She was a finned, thick-fleshed, water-breathing sea kynd.

Perhaps she had their magic.

Desperate to find some kind of defense before the queen arrived, Vahly tried to recall the spell the guard had spoken over her, the one that gave energy.

"Na gemísei me sthénos," she whispered.

A bolt of strength surged through her, pounding in her

blood as the sound of crashing waves echoed in her ears. Her fins tingled with the feel of…what?

Magic.

Had to be.

This was water kynd's power. Through spells spoken in their language and the sea's essence in their blood, they could swim like the swiftest fish, throw their spears into the hearts of their foes, and call back the weapons at will.

And now Vahly could do that too.

Well, if she could learn more spells. She sagged. Hope had lit her up, but now she realized learning more spellwork would be anything but an easy solution. The guard had been a fool to speak so loudly and clearly in front of her. When Ryton had worked his magic, he'd whispered, his words inaudible.

Vahly raised her head to call the foolish guard back, to get more from him, but a haunting voice annihilated that plan.

"So glad you're awake, little Earth Queen." Astraea had arrived.

CHAPTER NINE

Nix flew alongside Kyril, their wings flapping in rhythm, matching pace in the piercing rays of the rising sun. The gryphon was larger than Nix now, so big that it was nearly unthinkable.

Though she'd never admit it, it had been nice having him nearby as they'd flown through the night. Vahly's capture had truly shaken Nix to the bone. She wasn't sure why she'd never thought the sea kynd could get their hands on Vahly, but honestly, she'd thought everything would work out, that they would win the day. Especially after the new magic Kyril had given to Vahly with their bonding. Green fire to back up dragonfire? How could their enemies stand against it?

But now, with Vahly leagues away, buried in water…

Kyril squawked and veered toward Nix, gently brushing a feathered wing against her own reptilian one. She gave him a nod.

You're a good one, gryphon. I should come up with a nickname for you.

Kyril suddenly dipped and began a quick descent.

Had she upset him?

But then Nix saw exactly why he was flying toward the ground like a falling star. The scrub-and-vine strewn mountains led into a ravine that surrounded the plateau on which the Forest of Illumahrah grew. Nix was fairly certain that ravine had been dry and covered in spindly trees. Now, sea water churned against the plateau, waves splashing into the ancient forest.

Nix's heart stuttered. What was this?

The forest—the oldest on the island, the one the elves had called home since the beginning of time, the very birthplace of all life where the original Blackwater rested in the Source's primary spring—lay in ruins.

It wasn't even her homeland, but the pain of this loss filled her bones, cracking marrow and shunting pain from head to tail. Astraea had attacked the elves. With spelled salt water and thundering waves, she'd swamped the plateau. And while the water had mostly sloughed off now, the damage was done, leaving only a blackened mess of what had been a peaceful, thriving civilization.

Had the Sea Queen struck because she knew Arc was helping Vahly, the Earth Queen, the only one capable of gaining power equal to hers?

Without the elves, Arc had no one to join him in aiding Vahly in her escape from the sea. Was he now the last of his kynd like Vahly? Tears pricked Nix's eyes.

They had to see if there were any survivors.

If Cassiopeia had made it through, there was still hope for Arc's plan to rip Vahly from the sea kynd's grip.

Nix slid into a glide beside Kyril. In their two shadows,

immense oaks lay like grass flattened by a storm's wind. Wide-leafed ferns, wildflowers, and mosses sat in heaps, sending the smell of mildew and rot into the early autumn breeze.

Kyril shook his dark, feathered head and flew west. Nix trailed him, taking up an air current that seemed too kind and gentle to exist above such horror.

Below, hundreds of bloating corpses littered the forest floor. The stench gripped Nix's snout and turned her stomach.

We need to search for their queen, Kyril. Pale hair. Powerful.

Tasting the sour wind, Nix considered what the gryphon might or might not understand. But it wouldn't hurt to inform him. Heart breaking for Arcturus and what this meant for him, Nix scanned Illumahrah for any movement.

But there was nothing. Aside from the rustle of leaves crusted with salt and curling as they died, not a sound issued from the earth.

When would Arc arrive in Tidehame? Nix wondered if she should leave now and try to fly over the sea kynd's civilization to attempt to speak telepathically with Arc and inform him that he would be without further aid from his kynd.

Kyril veered southward, and Nix stayed just behind him. No, she couldn't give up just yet. If there were any who'd lived through this, they needed aid now. No food or drinkable water would be found in this disaster. No healing from their fellow kynd. This might be the only chance to find and save the last of Arc's kynd. They had to keep searching.

Head for the Source's spring, Nix said to Kyril. *The Blackwater.*

LEAGUE AFTER LEAGUE THEY FLEW, BACK AND FORTH, zigzagging across the plateau on their way to the spring, witnessing the devastation. Silver pines snapped into halves and drawn into circles by whirlpools. Boulders dragged through deep mud by what had to have been incredibly powerful currents driven by water magic. Elven bodies with bright hair dashed against rocks. The elves' younglings torn limb from limb, the teeth marks of sea monsters visible as Nix and Kyril swooped low to check for survivors. More dead, some who looked only to be sleeping peacefully, their eyes closed forever, hands outstretched as if reaching for one another in their final moments.

Finally, Nix nudged Kyril with her wing tip and headed for a landing place near what had once been the royal palace. Wing joints aching and her old wounds pulsing, she dropped from the sky beside Kyril. The gryphon shook out his massive wings, then tucked them by his sides. The tree palace looked like an emptied husk, velvets and sparkling jewels spilling from its broken walls. Inside, floodwaters had stripped the floors bare of the carpets of moss and fine fabrics. There was no sign of the long table that had sat in the great hall. No more scrolls like the ones Vahly had told Nix about.

Nix transformed and grabbed a wine-colored tunic that had snagged on a branch against the oaken palace. The salt water had crusted the fabric, but it was whole enough to serve. She ripped two openings for her wings. The clasp at the neck had been roughed up, but it held. A shudder hit her as she pulled the garment over her head and wings. The spells would be long gone, so the water wouldn't hurt her, but still, the scent, the feel of the salt...

She shook again before calling out. "We are here to help! Is anyone here?" The smell was horrifying. She took up a corner of the long tunic and held it over her nose.

Kyril walked behind her, clucking worriedly. Nix glanced at him over her shoulder. His feathers and twitching lion's tail brushed the fallen trees and stone debris that crowded the way from the palace to the spring.

He let out a plaintive screech.

Nix stepped over a muddied collection of wooden bowls and red berries, a crushed archery target, and a glittering array of crystal. Had the Blackwater spring survived this? Would it be tainted with spelled salt water?

As if in answer to her unspoken question, the scent of the Source's spring danced through the terrible odors, cleansing and calming, leading the way.

The stones around the spring lay in disarray, but there in the center was the Blackwater, sparkling black with hints of Lapis blue, fire red, and gold.

She gave Kyril a sad smile. "Well, at least some things remain."

Kyril settled himself beside the pool of sacred water. He tucked his legs underneath himself like a mountain cat, and if they hadn't been through such a day, Nix would have told him to sit more grandly as befits a flying creature. The gryphon eyed her with large eyes, his head high above hers.

For such a peaceful place, the Forest of Illumahrah had

crushing sadness for Nix. She felt the presence of Dramour, Ibai, and Kemen. Their loss would never be far from her mind.

Lifting her gaze from the dazzling spring and its whispering power, she eyed the surrounding debris. "Anyone? We cannot stay. Please call out if you are alive. We are friends."

The wind rose and tossed a strand of her red hair over her shoulder, where it caught on the tunic's clasp. She started to work the tangle, then froze.

"Kyril, did you hear that?"

He perked up, swiveling his head in the direction of the noise.

Nix walked past the spring. It had barely been anything to note. A short punch of hollow sound like someone had struck a broken bell. Twigs strangled in seaweed snapped underfoot and sand found its way between Nix's toes. Gritting her teeth against these reminders of the sea folk, she wound her way through two trees that had been twisted together by the spelled waves, their branches like reaching claws.

Kyril growled, going still beside her.

On a hill just above them, a cave spilled out three forms.

CHAPTER TEN

As the Sea Queen swam through the barred door, Vahly would've held her breath if she knew how in this new body. What would Astraea want to hear from her and how long would she let Vahly live in an effort to gain this information?

Vahly sat straight, not bothering to hide the fact that the ginger-haired guard had untied all but one of her bindings. Astraea wasn't the type of opponent one tried to sneak things past. The Sea Queen wore the cool expression and calm demeanor of a female fully in charge of her surroundings and her future as she dismissed the guard, locked the door with her spear, and turned to face Vahly.

Vahly would need to pull an Ace out of thin air—or water—to survive this day.

First step, unsettle the opponent by revealing an unexpected and powerful card.

"When your lover changed me into one of you, he gave me sea magic. Isn't that something?" Vahly grinned, enjoying her bluff. Astraea didn't need to know that Vahly had zero idea how to use said magic. Let her wonder if Vahly could call up a wave as well as any.

Astraea's red lips parted, her eyes widening.

Success. Vahly had chipped the cold exterior of this queen.

But Astraea schooled her features and returned Vahly's grin. "General Ryton was operating under my orders, little queen."

Step two, study the opponent in action.

So Astraea was going to play as though giving Vahly magic was part of the plan. Vahly knew full well it had not been as she said. Ryton had almost killed Vahly before changing her. The indecision in his eyes had told the story. The Sea Queen may have sent Ryton after Vahly, but more than just loyalty had been swimming through Ryton's head during the capture and subsequent spellwork. He had been tortured by something deep inside his heart. Vahly had seen as much from battle-scarred dragons. The behavior was familiar.

Astraea whispered, words inaudible, her gaze above Vahly's head. Vahly twisted to see a golden, legless creature slip out of a crack in the wall. Vahly's mind sifted through possible reasons that Astraea would call up an impossibly long fish that moved like a snake. The thing's scales glittered in the dim prison as it circled Vahly.

"Have you heard of a coinfish?"

The fish curled around Vahly's ankles, the touch light and gritty like sand.

"Can't say that I have." Despite her cavalier words, Vahly's stomach tightened with fear.

"Your kynd used to travel across our ocean on ships,"

Astraea said, her accent extending the S sound and clipping the words at odd places. "Sometimes they were careless with the gold coin they carried. When it dropped into the sea, lightning eels gobbled them up. Eventually, these gold-eaters became something new entirely. Coinfish."

The fish uncurled and slithered through the water that flowed between Astraea and Vahly. Vahly fisted her hands, trying to control her fear.

Time for step three: play a card that makes the opponent believe they're winning.

It wasn't tough to find a good whimper and let it out. Vahly's sound of trepidation brought the smile back to Astraea's horrible, beautiful face.

"Place this on your tongue, little queen, and we will have a lesson in determination. Coinfish are known for their tenacity." Astraea held out a circle of gold. It was a human coin.

Vahly's heart stumbled around her chest like a newborn dragon.

The Sea Queen shoved the coin between Vahly's lips. Astraea whispered as she pinched Vahly's cheeks, forcing Vahly to swallow the gold, "They're such hungry beasts."

Skin heating like another high fever had taken her, Vahly choked the coin down. "You can't get information from a corpse," she spat out, gagging and keeping an eye on the circling coinfish.

Astraea stepped back, her webbed toes stirring up sand. After adjusting her scarlet coral and gold crown, she crossed her arms over her pearl-encrusted dress. "The coinfish won't kill you, little queen. It will only make you beg for death. They can live inside a host for days on end."

As the coinfish undulated toward Vahly's mouth, she imagined growing scales like a dragon. She envisioned the steely scales covering her insides, shielding her emotions, waking up her mind. She refused to die like this. No daughter of Amona the Lapis Matriarch would go down in such a low and twisted way. No. No. No.

She locked her jaw as the fish struck at her face with its sharp teeth. Pain cut across her lips and down her chin.

Then water blasted into Vahly, and Astraea cackled, her spear outstretched. Vahly's mouth was blown wide open. The coinfish slid into Vahly's mouth, down her throat, into her stomach.

The world blurred. Pain bloomed in every part of her body as she heaved, trying to dislodge the beast from her stomach. The beast was a sword in her belly, slicing, burning, destroying her from the inside out. She doubled over, but that only made the pressure in her body build and made her feel as though her head were about to explode like a pocket of torched sulfur.

"Don't worry," Astraea cooed. "Once he has eaten the coin, he will calm down. Until he grows hungry again."

But Vahly could barely hear Astraea over the pounding in her veins. Her earth magic thrashed deep within her, panicked and smothered by the sea's power and the change in Vahly's body. The earth magic wanted to save her, to help, but Vahly couldn't comprehend anything except the blinding agony.

Then the beast was silent and still inside her.

"See?" Astraea raised a palm. "You lived. You are strong. And now you will tell me exactly where Amona sleeps."

Vahly shivered, pain making the colors of Astraea's crown and the features of her face go hazy and indistinct. Vahly's new gills shuddered, opening and closing in an uneven rhythm that had her gasping for breath in a place with no air. An errant thought slid into her head. Why hadn't the coinfish gone after the gold in Astraea's crown? Only coins must tempt it. Her mind spun, random thoughts riding the haze of pain. Arc would say the coinfish had fascinating behavioral developments.

"Amona sleeps…" A cough tore at her throat and she gagged. "In the Lapis palace."

Astraea rolled her eyes. "Where exactly? On a lower level? Or near the western entrance? Or does she prefer to look out across the territory of those she kills, perched on the cliffs like a filthy, stinking harbinger of death?"

If Vahly gave them this information, the sea folk would tweak their flooding plans, making certain to strike Amona's chambers. Presumably at night. But if Vahly could escape and warn them, maybe even set up a surprise attack from the northern reaches on the night Astraea struck out, the dragons could win the day.

"What makes you think I would tell you the truth?"

"I can spot a lie, child."

Astraea wouldn't spot Vahly's lie. She'd spent a lifetime bluffing and fibbing her way around the cider house, the Jade palace, and even in her own Lapis home during pranks and jobs done with Nix and the others.

Nauseated from the coinfish that had started turning in her stomach, Vahly envisioned Dramour as he bluffed at the cards table, her heart aching with the memory of her lost friend. He made direct eye contact when lying, his grin a prequel to a mocking chuckle. Vahly did her best to mimic the display.

"Her chambers are on the floor above the feasting hall." She paused as the coinfish jerked suddenly and pain cracked her composure for a moment. Taking a shuddering breath, she continued, "Near the tunnel leading from the western entrance." It was almost true. Near truths made the best lies. Amona actually slept on the higher levels above the hall.

The Sea Queen studied Vahly with darting glances toward her eyes, mouth, and the set of her shoulders. "Good. For your reward, I will make the next question quick."

"How is that a reward, exactly?"

"The sooner we complete this questioning, the sooner you get to die and end the pain of having the coinfish in your belly."

It was a sad fact that death did seem like a positive right now. Vahly hugged her free hand to her middle.

"How many dragons live in the Lapis palace?"

Honestly, Vahly had no idea. But fewer dragons meant less water in the attack, right? "A little over five hundred."

Astraea's grin was a sharpened blade.

If Vahly didn't play step four soon in this game, if she didn't play her winning hand soon, death would welcome her into the darkness.

The coinfish lurched, and Vahly thrashed, her insides twisting and spasming like she was being squeezed by a pair of giant hands. Dots swam in the green-gray water before her eyes.

"Time for a snack." Astraea produced another coin and shoved it down Vahly's throat with a finger.

Choking and bucking, Vahly fought hard, trying not to swallow. She bit down on Astraea's finger, and the Sea Queen yelped and pulled back as blood spread like fire. Tasting the gold of the coin sliding down her throat and the metallic tang of the queen's blood, Vahly steeled herself for the agony of the coinfish's feasting.

But a tingling spread through her mouth and down her neck, and the sound of water magic roared in her ears. Squeezing her eyes shut, she focused her will on the beast in her belly.

Out. Out. Out.

Invisible waves crashed in Vahly's ears, and she felt strong, strong enough to fight Astraea's creature.

Go. Go. Go.

The beast wriggled up Vahly's throat, fins slicing her from the inside as it swam from her mouth.

When Vahly opened her eyes, Astraea's face was contorted with shock, her mouth drawn back from her white teeth and her stare blank.

Another coin flashed between Astraea's fingers.

Vahly imagined water rushing forward, and the sea obeyed, coursing at Astraea and pushing her back a step. The Sea Queen shrieked, then lunged at Vahly, coin in hand. The beast whipped through the water above their heads, and Vahly pulled against her binding, the sea rope cutting into her wrist as she rose to meet Astraea. Anger and the desperate need to survive raced through her veins as she raised a hand to grab the Sea Queen.

"Déno," Astraea whispered.

Something sharp wrapped around Vahly's formerly free arm and yanked her backward, slamming her onto the rock shelf and jarring her teeth together. Stunned, Vahly's mouth popped open. She shut it quickly. A second coinfish surrounded her arm, holding her tight. Vahly lifted both knees and launched her feet into the Sea Queen's middle. Astraea stumbled back a step before snarling and rushing forward, her face in Vahly's. The scent of the Sea Queen's magic flowed across Vahly's gills: salt, blood, and an overpowering floral reek like rotted blooms.

Gold danced between Astraea's fingers. She was going to ram that coin down Vahly's throat.

This was it. Vahly wouldn't survive.

CHAPTER ELEVEN

Ryton finished his lean meal of scallops infused with sour coralweed and looked out the window of his bedroom. His hands shook, and he knew why. The Earth Queen, the one he had been ordered to kill, the true enemy of his kynd and friend to the one who had murdered his sister, had surprised him by being…likable.

She'd been like one of his own. Courageous. A personality touched by dark humor. Tenacious.

And he'd been unable to end her terrible march toward overpowering Astraea and slaying the sea kynd. Ryton's brother would have fought Ryton over this. After all, on his deathbed, he'd made Ryton swear to avenge Selene, and permitting the Earth Queen—the one who could ensure the dragons' final win over the sea kynd—to live certainly wasn't upholding his oath. Ryton swallowed, the taste of scallops bitter at the back of his throat. Passing his hammock, he lifted the carved image that showed him and his siblings when they were young. He ran a finger over their eyes, their smiles.

"I failed you. I wish I could tell you why," he whispered. "I wish you could be here, that you could see this Earth Queen, that you could know how very much like us she truly is." It was shocking. An abhorrent thought. But it was the truth, and he couldn't deny it. She didn't seem like a monster. He wished she did. It would've made his mission so much easier.

The brass bell outside his front door clanged.

Frowning, he swam through the bedroom and living quarters. Who would be visiting him now? He'd heard Grystark was gone on some mission. No one else bothered with Ryton, as he'd designed his life to one of service, not socializing.

When he swung the door open, it wasn't Grystark, but Grystark's wife, Lilia. She was dressed in an unusually drab color, and her eyes were swollen and pink. Scars laced her cheeks in pale stripes.

He pulled her into a hug. "What happened? Who did this to you?" She was healed and had been for a while.

Shaking her head, she started to speak but stopped, her chin trembling. "What is this?" Grimacing, she touched one leg of the black beast, a joint that crossed his collarbone.

"Don't fret. I will be through with it soon enough. It was a part of my mission."

His failed mission. He was lying to Lilia. He knew well he'd never rid himself of the creature that hissed in his mind and morphed his body into a land kynd when necessary. He'd almost grown used to the pain of its dark presence, the pulling at his heart and soul. And for what had he given up his normal life? He hadn't killed the Earth Queen. It had been a waste.

"Please, tell me who attacked you." He touched her cheek gently, his stomach turning as he imagined the pain she must have been in. "Was it an accident?"

Lilia blinked, staring at the thing on Ryton's back, but it was obvious her distress went beyond that. "You, you don't know," she stammered. "That's why you haven't searched for me. You truly don't know. I didn't believe she would hold it from you. I didn't think she could. But—"

"What is it? Come in. Tell me everything."

He gestured to a stool, but she didn't sit. Whispering to herself, she paced over the knotted rug, bubbles caught in her hair and streaming around her fingers and ankles.

"Lilia. You're scaring me. And that's no small thing. Please, tell me. I'm here for you and Grystark, no matter the situation."

She spun and gripped his forearms, her fingers biting into his flesh. Her mouth turned down at the edges and quivered. "The queen, she made the army take your tunnel to attack the elves."

"I know. I imagine it was a difficult trip under the isle. The tunnel wasn't yet ready."

"He's gone, Ryton. Grystark is dead."

Ryton's ears rang like Lilia had clanged the outside bell a thousand times.

He'd heard her wrong.

"No."

"Ryton." She gasped, bowing her head. "Yes, he is dead. Our Grystark is dead."

Ryton stared at her weeping form, his mind rushing to the tunnel he'd designed, envisioning how dark it had been and how the cracking of the bedrock above had sounded like a monstrous squid from the wide, open waters.

"She demanded that they go when she knew it wasn't ready." Lilia beat her hands on Ryton's chest, her hair coming undone and her eyes wild. "Echo told me everything. How he warned her and how the ceiling had already begun to fall when she ordered him to lead the charge, to continue onward. She didn't care. She doesn't care that she killed one of her greatest generals and fifty-three of her own soldiers. We lost fewer warriors in our last attack. Queen Astraea is no better than a filthy, soulless dragon!"

Ryton pulled her head against him and ran a hand over her back, trying to calm her frantic sobbing. Words refused to rise to his lips. His heart froze over like the waters in the far northern realms.

Lilia allowed herself to be led to his hammock. Ryton tucked her in like she was a child, giving her an overlarge kelp blanket and promising her he wouldn't leave, that they would talk more after she'd rested.

"The queen gave me these scars when Gry argued with her," Lilia whispered. "But they are nothing compared to..." Her shoulders shook as she wept.

Normally, Lilia would never permit Ryton, or anyone, to treat her like this, comforting her and coddling her. But she seemed beyond argument, taking the comfort he offered like a starving creature would a morsel of food.

Propping himself against the wall to keep an eye on her, he allowed what she had said to wash over him like a red tide, filled with noxious growth and stinging nettles.

Grystark, his one and only friend, had died.

In the tunnels, where Astraea had demanded Grystark go, he had been crushed by rock, pummeled and smothered by Ryton's own creation.

Ryton's heart remained frozen. He couldn't feel the loss. But distantly, he knew the pain would arrive with lashing claws to rip him apart.

He felt as though he'd been bound and thrown into Scar Chasm to fall and fall, forever in the darkness.

LILIA WOKE, GAVE RYTON ONE LAST HUG, THEN LEFT, SAYING she had a safe place to stay with a friend, a place out of Astraea's sight.

Ryton's heart thawed, then began to catch fire. Like the horrible dragons' flames, it sparked and burned. Shaking with rage, he took up his spear.

Astraea may have been his queen. He may have made an oath. But she had broken all ties by sending Grystark to his death and treating the loss as something that could be hidden away, tucked into a convenient place until she was ready to reveal it.

Ryton blasted through his door and into the open sea.

The sea kynd could deal with the dragons on their own. They didn't need this mad tyrant. Now, nothing would hold Ryton back.

Astraea would pay.

CHAPTER TWELVE

Nix lifted her head to speak to the elves who had emerged from the cave on the hill. "Who is there? We're friends, not foe. Don't be afraid."

She remembered two of the three elves, ones Vahly and Arc had introduced. The first was Haldus, short for an elf, with brown hair and a steady gaze. He'd been a warrior and a steward of sorts for the royal family. Behind Haldus was Rigel with his flinty head of thick hair and gaze like a hawk. The last elf seemed slightly familiar, but Nix didn't remember meeting her.

The elves, eyes sunken with grief and hunger, bowed politely to Nix and Kyril.

Rigel spoke first, his tone flat. Nix recognized his suppressed emotion and her heart went out to him.

"Greetings, Mistress of the Dragon's Back." Rigel turned to Kyril. "May I ask where you met this fine gryphon? We've not seen one in an age."

"Forgive my bluntness," Nix said. "But shouldn't we be searching for survivors?"

Haldus swallowed. "There are no more. It is only us."

Nix pressed a fist against her stomach, feeling overwhelmed. "Forgive me once again, but if you have no immediate need, we do. One of the sea folk captured the Earth Queen."

Rigel and Haldus exchanged a panicked glance. The female stepped forward. Her grass-green gown had been ripped at the hem and along one sleeve. Her golden hair hung lank over her thin shoulders. Nix could've blown her away with one breath.

"Please allow me to help." The elf's gaze darted from Nix to Kyril.

Rigel shook his head. "This is Ursae. She supported Mattin fully and fought against us during that terrible time. You cannot trust her."

Fury drew a sword inside Nix's chest, longing to strike out at this elf, this creature who might well have assisted in murdering Dramour, Ibai, and Kemen. Smoke curled from Nix's nostrils and mouth.

Ursae's cheeks reddened "I want to make amends."

Haldus ignored her. "Where is Arcturus?"

Kyril keened and spread his wings, though he remained on the ground. He showed Nix an image of Arc diving into the sea. The scene pushed Nix's anger to the back of her mind.

"What is it?" Rigel asked, Kyril's beating wings shuffling his silver hair.

"There is no time to explain," Nix said. "Arcturus went into the sea after Vahly."

The elves' eyes widened, and Haldus put a hand on Rigel's shoulder, fingers gripping tightly.

Rigel tugged his salt-crusted tunic straight. "Well, we will join him. To Tidehame, I suspect?"

Nix nodded. "So you have the magic to accomplish a sea journey?"

Ursae began walking quickly. "Because we are the first people, our magic is not as hindered by salt water and the ocean's power like yours and the human's. Come. The sea is this way. Do you believe the Earth Queen still lives?"

"I hope." Nix's pulse tripped. "I don't know why he chose to take her instead of killing her when he had the chance. It almost seemed as though he warred with the idea himself."

"The sea kynd wasn't sure whether to kill her or not?" Rigel asked as they crawled over a broken oak the size of the entire cider house.

"That's what it seemed like to me. I'm a pretty good judge of character, of behavior," Nix said. "But I don't know how they could even keep her alive, human as she is."

Rigel stumbled upon a corpse, and they all paused, wincing and shutting their eyes for a moment against the bloated and torn body. He took a breath and led them onward, outpacing Ursae. "They have magic enough to do as they see fit under the waves."

"Well, don't waste a moment walking with us. We're worthless under the water. Do your elven magic and get there to him as quickly as you are able. I am so sorry for your loss here and what the Sea Queen has done to your kynd. Please know we hate to interrupt your grieving."

Rigel halted the group. "Thank you for your kind words. We will use our magic to find Arcturus before the sun has set on this day. I swear it," he said, facing Kyril and bowing deeply. "I will inform Queen Vahly that her familiar lives on and is ready for the fight."

Kyril raised himself onto his back legs, lion claws digging into the muddy debris. He squawked, the sound deafening. It was an agreement of sorts, or at least that was how Nix saw it.

Nix touched Rigel's arm. "Thank you for doing what I cannot for my friend. She is dear to me beyond her fated duty." Her words broke, and she stifled a sob. Vahly's body might already be floating dead in the sea. Or the sea folk might be torturing her, flooding her lungs with salt water. Nix could almost see Vahly's light eyes going wide with pain. Nix swallowed, feeling sick.

Rigel put his hand over Nix's, his flesh pale against her blue scales. "I understand."

Swallowing, Nix thought of what she and Kyril might be able to accomplish here on land. "Vahly told us that her magic was drawing her to the Lost Valley, to the place of her birth. When you rescue her, help her reach that place. She has something to do there with Kyril, we believe. I will travel to see the Lapis on our way to the Lost Valley, and I will inform Matriarch Amona about what has happened to this place and to our Earth Queen. Perhaps she will have more help to offer."

Rigel pressed his lips together and nodded. He stepped back and began to disappear.

"Grief must wait," Haldus said, his voice tinged with sadness and his body shimmering out of view along with Rigel's and Ursae's.

As soon as they were gone, Nix longed to leave this place, its horror and stench. "Come on, Kyril. We have some bad news to break to a very angry dragon queen. It's best to get these things over with as quickly as possible."

Her wry tone covered her increasing fear for Vahly. If she lost her girl, she wasn't sure she could keep on fighting. Without Vahly, she was pretty certain her heart would refuse to beat.

CHAPTER THIRTEEN

Vahly thrashed against Astraea's hold, the Sea Queen's water magic crushing her chest and filling her ears with the roaring sound of so much power. Vahly's bones felt weak and brittle, like at any second they would snap and jab through her flesh, white daggers thrust from inside.

"Stop!" A booming voice crossed the currents. Ryton stood, spear raised, at the closed door to the cell, his eyebrows drawn together and the muscles in his arms and legs seemingly coiled, ready to spring.

What was he doing? Could this be good? A bit of dissension in the ranks?

Turning to face Ryton, Astraea kept the water rushing at Vahly to hold her in place. "Polyagapiménos. Xéro óti den dósate móno sti vasílissa sas parangelía," Astraea said in the sea folk tongue, her grin sharp and her tone syrupy.

Vahly's stomach burned with the damage the coinfish had done. The fish swam around her head and blocked her view of Ryton for a moment before swimming into the dark water above the rock shelf. Its smaller cohort joined it, and they squirmed and knotted like shimmering snakes.

Ryton's only answer was a spell. "Katastréfo!" Magic crackled from the tip of his spear.

The coral branches of the cell's opening exploded in a cloud of debris.

But the blast didn't alter Astraea's position at all. Her lips moved as Ryton charged inside, his gaze going to the coinfish. He reached into a pocket at his belt as a current streamed from Astraea toward him. Shouting and dropping his spear, he fell to his knees against the remains of the door. Astraea advanced on him, still whispering spells. The water around Ryton glittered like sapphires, a shape like a net closing in, tighter and tighter.

And then the pressure on Vahly's body relented. Astraea was distracted by her lover's betrayal. Now was the moment to act.

Vahly knew she couldn't outswim Astraea or her army. The coin Astraea had been threatening Vahly with lay on the mosaic floor, but it was out of reach, bound as she was by one wrist.

Summoning that roaring magic newly sewn into her being and poured into her blood, Vahly mimicked Ryton's spell, focusing on the rubbery plant that held her tight.

"Katastréfo," she whispered.

Her binding snapped and she lunged for the coin. Ryton was groaning. Blood pooled at every point where the net touched his skin. He was going to die—and die badly.

Vahly swam up behind Astraea, who was so focused on disciplining her general that she took no notice. Vahly gripped the hair tangled in Astraea's crown, yanked the Sea Queen's head back, and jammed the coin between her lips.

Astraea spit the coin into the water and shrieked a spell, her bloodshot eyes as wide as a dragon's.

Vahly swam for the opening, heart and stomach rolling and falling and failing. Black spots danced in front of her eyes as pain cut her deeply. Outside the cell, the ground dropped away. She was hundreds of feet above the sea's floor. She'd never been near bedrock. Astraea had guessed what Vahly's earth magic might have been able to accomplish.

A tumbling rush of water hit Vahly like the wind of a violent storm, and she spun backward.

Ryton and Astraea shouted in their language, thunder rocking the sea around them. Vahly's head banged against the tower cell. The world flickered to tones of gray. She blinked, hurting everywhere, and tried to rotate in the water, to get a handle on what to do and what resources there might be at her disposal before the distraction of Ryton's fight was gone and she'd missed the opportunity to escape.

The sea stretched, empty and deep, far, far into the distance. Vahly braced bleeding hands on the tower wall as Ryton shrieked in pain again. Beyond the tower, there was a palace made of the same scarlet coral as the cell door had been. Probably Astraea's own home. Not a fine place to escape. But there were outbuildings nearby. Where could Vahly go? Maybe there. But she might flee right into a unit of more guards. She needed a place to hide and plan. She closed her eyes. There was no time. And how long would she even live with this kind of internal damage?

But there was no other idea in her head.

Wishing she could help Ryton now that he'd proven he wasn't who she'd thought him to be, she swam away from the tower.

Guards called out behind her.

Vahly sucked the water through her gills and envisioned the water magic rushing around her, helping her onward. Roaring currents filled her ears as she sped toward a row of outbuildings beyond the palace's outer wall.

She shot through what looked like a stable, its walls carved out of the same rock as the shelf in the cell. It was empty, and as she rushed through one door and out another, her speed stirred up sand and squares of harvested seaweed that had been stacked into a corner. The stable led to a covered courtyard. Twelve doors like the one she'd just been through stood around the pebbled ground. A ceiling of pearly shell boasted an array of glowing lights like green and white torches. But they looked like turtles or…

She had no time to study them. Picking a door to the right, she tucked herself into a corner and stacked the cut seaweed blocks around her.

A sound made her jump, her poor body trembling.

Eyes the color of sunset, like Amona's, blinked in the darkness, luminous. A head emerged, horse-like, but where a mane would have been, fins lined the creature's neck. The body dipped low and curled, ending in a tail. The thing had no limbs at all, but it did have a mouth, and Vahly worried it might be like many other sea beasts. Hungry.

She shuffled back, pressing into the corner so as not to appear threatening and keeping an eye on the door for the approaching guards. Their voices echoed in the rippling water.

Vahly took a handful of the seaweed and held it out. "I would leave you to your room, but I'm afraid I can't pop out just now. I'm either dying or about to be killed. Either way, moving isn't in my plans. Sorry."

The beast swam forward. Wide fins on each of its sides moved like dragon wings. Extending its neck, it took the seaweed from her with a careful mouth. Its teeth were not scary, thank the Blackwater. They were flat and simple. A plant eater, then.

"Good. I've been nibbled on enough for one day." Vahly gave the thing another serving. She moved slowly, deliberately, to keep quiet.

The guards' voices came closer. Vahly froze, longing for Kyril like she'd left a limb on land.

If he were here, she would ride him to safety. He could protect her when she was down. Stones, he had to be so frightened in her absence, wondering what was happening to her. Their bond buzzed inside her blood, insistent as the magic's pull to the Lost Valley.

She was being torn apart by the desperation to go to Kyril and the absolute need to swear some oath or speak a spell of sorts with him at the place of her birth. She fisted her shaking hands as the seahorse—for that was what it resembled; a horse of the ocean—bumped Vahly gently, requesting another snack.

A thunderous boom sounded distantly, and sparkling sand shifted from the ceiling of the stable and fell over Vahly's hiding place. Shouts rose, the guards' voices falling away.

"What was that?" Vahly asked the seahorse, lamely wishing it could do more than ask for food.

Edging out of her corner, Vahly gripped the side of the doorway and peered into the covered courtyard. No guards swarmed the area. No one was there at all. She stood on wobbling legs.

Pain rose, clawing and sharp, and she collapsed on the sandy rock. But she couldn't sit here and die. She braced herself with a palm to the cold and gritty ground. Now was the time to swim away. Something had distracted the guards. This was her chance. Her only chance.

Trying to stand again, she coughed. Blood trickled from her lips and clouded the water around her face. She sagged against the doorframe and eyed the seahorse.

"There is a sad part of me that wishes you could swallow me up like you do that seaweed. I wouldn't mind all of this simply being over."

But she didn't truly mean that. Her soul glowed inside her, and now more than ever, she knew only she could save Nix, Amona, Arc, and Kyril. As impossible as it seemed, she was their sole chance at survival.

A blur of movement across the courtyard caught her eye, and she slid back into the darkness.

Then a face appeared in the doorway, and she shouted in shocked happiness.

"Arc!"

How was he here? She just couldn't absorb it. He looked like a sacred spirit, his skin luminescent, his eyes dark and powerful, his shirtless body filling the doorway, his grin sweet and sure.

He gathered her into his arms, then sat with her cradled

on his lap, the doorframe against his back. He felt warm and light and perfect. The bare skin of his chest, covering powerful muscles, sent heat into her body, and she wished she could soak it all in and somehow end up in a patch of sun on the land, away from all of this.

With a thumb, he wiped the blood from her mouth. His touch was a balm. His eyebrows knitted over his flashing eyes, and his upper lip twitched.

Who did this to you? His fingers hovered over her gills, then brushed her stomach, his elven senses most likely guiding him to her worst injuries. *That male sea kynd?*

"How did you make it this far?" Had she actually died? Because this couldn't be happening.

Magic, he said inside her mind.

She breathed water out like an exhale, her body relaxing.

Now, hold still, I must heal you.

It was Astraea's doing, Vahly said telepathically, gesturing to her injured mid-section. *Ryton, the male, ended up helping me escape.*

Arc cocked his head, disbelieving, as his hands wove magic over Vahly's body. Dark and light unspooled from his fingertips. He set a hand against her stomach and a pleasant, healing heat bloomed under his touch.

The pain faded into a dull ache before disappearing completely. It was surprising he could heal such a serious wound so quickly.

I wish I could call on my earth powers. In this form, the magic refuses to rise. How does your magic work so well in the sea?

Because we are the first kynd, elven magic works in all places, albeit to varying degrees. I am weaker here, but not completely ineffective. Especially now.

Now? Are you growing stronger?

I am. He frowned, the knowledge making him uncomfortable for some unknown reason.

But the questions would have to wait.

Vahly stood, wishing they had time for a proper thank you, then followed Arc out of the stall and into the glowing light of the courtyard.

Should I aid you in swimming? Arc asked.

No, when Ryton turned me into this, he accidentally gave me water magic. Watch this.

Vahly soared through the water, the sound of the sea kynd's magic crashing in her ears. She looked over her shoulder to see Arc swimming behind her, keeping up fairly well.

Elf, you are supposed to be far behind and incredibly impressed with me.

Shrugging, his lips quirking into a sly grin, he pulled his arms back, accomplishing a strong stroke as they exited the courtyard and swam into an empty side street.

A shout punched through the eddies curling around Vahly's head as she swam.

Her heart jumped.

Hurry! Arc came up beside her, increasing his speed, magic golden around his temples.

I will not be caught. Not again, she said, willing the words to become truth and doing her level best to shove the image of the coinfish from her thoughts.

CHAPTER FOURTEEN

Nix, in dragon form, and Kyril, wild with panic and flashing images to Nix every other minute, flew through a misty fog that cloaked the Lapis mountain palace. They'd traveled quickly over the fire marshes, only briefly using the resting spots Nix had found on her first trip across with Vahly. That felt like an age ago.

Nix and Kyril landed on the wide, stone steps, and Amona met them at the entrance.

"My scouts spotted you," Amona said, her voice tight. "What is it? What is happening?"

Nix changed into her human shape, but she'd been in such a hurry that she hadn't bothered saving her clothes during her earlier shift into full dragon form. Naked as the day she was born, she bowed slightly to Amona, too worried for Vahly to care if she was giving up some of her pride in greeting the matriarch as a subject would. "It's Vahly. The sea kynd took her."

Amona's face dropped into a mask of calm. She took a slow breath, smoke rising from her mouth and nose.

Tears burned Nix's eyes. A servant came from the entrance and handed her a long dress hemmed with the Lapis symbol.

"Did you fight for her?" Amona asked, her voice staccato. "Is there any way she could still be alive? Tell me everything."

Normally, Nix would gripe about that tone she was using, but she honestly didn't care right now. Plus she knew Amona was only questioning her in that way because she was afraid. Nix understood. She pulled her sleeves down to her wrists and jerked her chin at Kyril to follow her and Amona inside.

"There was no time for a fight. A male sea kynd came onto the shore and grabbed her while she was on the water's edge. I don't know how he managed it. Arcturus went after her."

"Good." Amona tilted her head as if she were communicating telepathically with another dragon. "Kyril," she said, glancing over her shoulder. "I am glad to see you so hale and hearty. Your queen will need you in the coming days."

So Amona was taking the positive outlook. Nix approved. It did no good to think the worst in this situation. They had to hope Arc would help Vahly escape. Somehow.

But how? Nix argued with herself silently. Vahly didn't have air magic like Arc. She couldn't breathe underwater.

Amona led them into the great hall where a feast was in progress. "Please, sit." She gestured to the seat next to what Nix assumed was Amona's own chair, then the matriarch waved her hand, gesturing that one of her nobles should make way for Nix.

The noble in question was a pale, sky blue color not often seen in dragons. There seemed to be a few younglings of that color though, and Nix privately wondered if the male had a bevy of lovers. The noble huffed at Amona's unspoken command, but with a look from Amona, he grimaced, bowed shallowly, and gave up his seat to Nix. He strode across the room to sit with some middle-aged warriors who were trading stories in loud voices.

Nix picked at her venison but couldn't manage to eat. "I have more bad news, Matriarch Amona. I'm afraid you're going to wish you'd left me on the steps."

Amona held her crystal goblet out for more cider. A servant flew a few feet above the goblet to pour and aerate the drink. "Do not hold back. The news is no fault of yours, I'm sure."

Such kind words from the Lapis matriarch. Times truly were changing.

"Astraea attacked Illumahrah."

Amona set her goblet on the table. "No."

"It is a disaster. The Source's spring remains, the Blackwater apparently unharmed. But the elven palace is hollowed out and severely damaged and..."

"Please. Tell me all. We must be prepared for the coming fight."

"It appears that all the elves, save three and Arcturus, are dead."

Amona slammed her goblet on the table and the dragons hushed, tucking their wings in submission, attentive to her anger. "Such allies. Gone." She closed her eyes and her chin dropped. Then she raised her head. "Please," she said to a passing servant, "take this away. Take everyone's away. We must hold off on such feasting." Pushing away from the table, she stood. "Our allies, the elves, have suffered a great loss at the hands of the sea folk. All the elves save four are gone from this world."

Hushed whispers crossed the hall as servants hurried to take the food back to the kitchens.

About half of the dragons filed out of the room, presumably heading for their chambers. Kyril had curled up in a corner of the great hall. His great blue-gray wings pulled around him like bed curtains.

Nix stood and faced Amona, who'd been giving directions to Helena, the healer who often worked with Vahly. Nix knew her from all of Vahly's tales.

"Matriarch Amona," Nix said, "the three remaining elves headed toward Tidehame in hopes of aiding Arc in his rescue efforts. I think we should gather a unit of yours and mine and head that way too. I can't stand not being a part of her rescue."

Amona nodded. "They might need help from the air. Please come to my chambers as soon as you—"

Then the sky blue noble at the warriors table made a gurgling sound and slid from his seat to the floor.

AFTER A GREAT AMOUNT OF CHAOS AND THE RETURN OF Helena, who had left when Amona had first announced the grave news, it was discovered that the noble, a Lord Maur, had contracted some terrible illness. It was eating his scales away at the edges, similar to what spelled salt water did but with more of a flaking effect rather than a blackening and dissolving one. But this sickness also brought a harsh fever and stole his desire for food.

Nix kept her distance, staying out of the way as Helena tried poultice after poultice, tonics, and salves. The smell of hyssop, yarrow, birch bark, and a thousand other herbs filled the great hall.

Then another Lapis, one of the warriors who had sat next to Lord Maur, also fell ill.

And a third.

A fourth.

Amona had the servants open the earthblood vents, her mask of calm firmly in place.

Nix found Kyril and sat beside him. "Come with me to the cider house." She stroked his enormous, terribly furry paw, and he tucked his beak under her arm. "We will get help for the Lapis and arrange a group to fly back to help our queen. All right?"

Kyril clicked his beak. He flashed an image of Vahly's open mouth and wide eyes, a memory he had of the moment she'd been taken. A small growling noise came from his belly.

"Are you hungry?" Nix fetched one of the plates of venison that had been set on a side table. She held it out for him, but he nudged it away and put his head under one of his wings.

Nix stood, hands on her hips. What was she supposed to do about this? How many challenges would they have at once?

Steeling herself, she kissed Kyril on the head and slipped out of the great hall. She needed back up. She needed her Call Breakers.

C H A P T E R   F I F T E E N

Vahly led Arc above the ocean city, the tower she'd been tortured in looming in the near distance.

Her earth magic pulsed inside her.

She stopped, hand to the spot beneath her heart, the place where she felt the tug to go to the Lost Valley and where she could almost feel her connection to Kyril, bright and burning.

What is it? A wrinkle appeared between Arc's eyebrows.

And then Vahly knew. *My earth magic is telling me to save General Ryton, the sea kynd male who rescued me. I don't understand, but I have to.* She searched Arc's features for an argument, but she only found his typical curiosity.

Who?

Ryton. He saved me. His queen threw some sort of horrible magical net over him up there. He gave himself up to free me. And my earth magic is telling me to keep him alive.

Two sea kynd guards with scarlet spears blasted from a three-level building. "Stop or die now!" they shouted in the dragon tongue.

We'll die anyway. Might as well go for it. Vahly upped her speed, begging this foreign power to answer to her will.

Agreed. But I'm going to attempt something, so swim in a straight line.

Arc spun inky darkness and sparkling light even as his legs kicked powerfully through the water.

Then he disappeared.

Vahly missed a stroke, turning.

Straight! Keep going! Arc was still there, just invisible.

Then his magic surrounded her, swathing her in light and a quiet hum that she hardly noticed over the earth magic drumming deep inside her and the water magic rushing through her blood and in her ears. She could still see her own body, but she supposed the guards couldn't see anything, because they both hung suspended, hovering and looking left and right, faces bunched in confusion.

Now, Arc whispered into her head. *To the tower, yes?*

He was such a good one. He didn't argue a bit about her wanting to rescue a mortal enemy. *Yes.*

Guards swarmed the area around the tower, their spears at the ready and their magic coursing through the chilly currents that passed across the cell's entrance.

Ryton lay on the floor of the broken prison cell. He shuddered as they swam inside, his body leaking blood from countless wounds. The net sparkled across his form, deep blue and pulled so tight that Ryton's flesh bulged between the strange fabric.

Arc made a growling sound inside Vahly's head. *What is on his back?*

I don't know. It has been with him the entire time.

Foul magic seeps from it. It is bent, wrong, very dark. I don't think we should touch it. At all.

Don't have to tell me twice. When she'd first seen the black creature riding Ryton's back, she'd thought perhaps it was just a sea kynd thing. But none of the others wore such a beast. Perhaps this was how Ryton had managed to crawl onto land.

The net lifted, seemingly of its own accord, but most likely because an invisible Arc was trying to cut an opening.

Ryton's eyes didn't open. He had no idea they were even there. His face was pale as milk, and his bones seemed to press against his bleeding skin. He did not look good. The male was not long for this world unless Arc had some kind of fantastic solution.

Is it cutting your skin? Vahly asked. There was too much blood in the water to be able to tell if Arc had injured himself as he tugged at the net.

A dagger appeared where she guessed Arc's hand worked. He sliced the net and began pulling it away from Ryton slowly, carefully. Vahly joined in, peeling the trap from her combination captor and savior.

Ryton groaned and blinked.

The net began to burn Vahly's fingers and palms. She hissed and pulled them back. *Arc,* she said warningly.

I know. It's burning me too. But I think we can get him out before it executes a deadly amount of damage. The magic feels as though it's very…focused.

Astraea spelled it just for him, hmm?

Seems that way, Arc said.

Well, they have a really interesting history, unless I'm mistaken.

Vahly went back to work alongside Arc, and finally they had the net completely separated from Ryton's shivering body.

I'm going to partially heal him now. Arc's deep voice was tight, full of nerves. *Will he try to kill us when he wakes from his stupor?*

Vahly kept an eye on the guards, who swam not twenty feet away. *I really hope not. That would put a damper on our escape.*

I only want to secure his survival, not completely mend him to his fullest capabilities, Arc said.

Vahly nodded even though none could see her. *Good plan.*

Rising onto an arm, Ryton opened his eyes, but they rolled back and he slumped forward again. There was a subtle shift in the cool water flowing across Vahly's face, then Ryton too disappeared.

I'll take his right arm, then you feel for us and grab his left, all right? Vahly moved forward, hands outstretched. Only Ryton's blood remained to mark where he'd been.

But you must avoid contact with that foul thing he carries.

I don't know if we can. Well, maybe if I put an arm around his waist and just have his arm over my neck.

When they had him securely supported, they shifted him out of the cell and started off, dodging guards and keeping quiet. Hopefully, Ryton would remain hazy and silent. If he woke, well, she didn't want to think about fighting him in his own element and trying to explain that they were only there to help. Oh, and there was the invisible thing. Yeah, it could get very tricky.

Vahly glanced over her shoulder, watching for guards.

But none trailed them. Not a one.

This is too easy, she said.

Vahly, I adore you, but you can keep that opinion to yourself. Maintaining the magic necessary to swim and breathe down here as well as healing both of you and speeding through this nightmarish place is far from simple.

Oh, Arc. I'm so sorry. You're right. I just feel like you're invincible.

I am not, sadly.

Let me take Ryton. With this new body, I am fine to carry him. Swimming is like walking.

Vahly, do you feel you can reverse this change in you once we make it to land?

She winced. *I have no idea.*

After swimming in silence for an eternity, Arc's breath began to sound in Vahly's head.

Are you all right?

Tired. A bit tired.

It was all the magic he was doing. *Let go of the invisibility. We're out of their city and haven't seen a warrior or guard in a while.*

Arc and Ryton shimmered into view. Arc's mouth hung open like he was panting as he swam.

The rocky northern coastline, most likely a spot near the Jade palace, showed black and turbulent not four hundred feet away.

Vahly's heart surged, and she tried to speak telepathically to Kyril. *Kyril, I am alive. I will see you soon.*

Her throat convulsed. She'd thought for a while that she would never see her familiar again.

But there was no answering image as was his form of communication. Still he was too far away. Or perhaps it was the water or her form.

Stones and Blackwater, please let me find a way to change back.

Arc hissed a warning as three figures swam out of the dark depths to the south, just behind them, aiming right at Arc.

CHAPTER SIXTEEN

*S*wim *to the surface, Arc. I'll fight them while you drag Ryton to land, then you can come back and help me out. I think I can use water magic against them.*

Taking Ryton from her, Arc began to speak, but then stopped. His brow wrinkled. *Vahly. They are my kynd.*

Vahly stopped trying to remember the spell Ryton had used to blast her cell open. *What?*

Elves. They are elves.

And sure enough, Rigel, Haldus, and a nasty female named Ursae who had been truly terrible in the aftermath of Mattin's death swam forward.

Vahly's heart lifted as hope sprang to life in Arc's tired eyes.

Telepathically, Arc explained quickly, and then they made for the rocky shore, all making certain not to touch the foul creature on Ryton's back.

The water was warmer here, nearer to the surface where the sun's rays bled life into the gray-blue world.

With the strength their kynd was known for, the elves

dragged Ryton across the broken rocks, up the sandy rise, and onto the land, their feet splashing Vahly's face as she broke the surface just behind them. The light seared her vision, throwing streaks of red against the backs of her eyelids as she winced. But the air was velvet. Instinctively, she tried to take a breath. Her throat closed up and her gills spasmed. Spots formed in front of her eyes. She couldn't breathe here. Of course she couldn't. She was a sea kynd.

Shuddering and fighting panic, she lowered her head beneath the lapping waves and took in what her new body needed in the water. Her gills relaxed, but her heart flapped erratically like a broken dragon wing.

I don't know how to change back, she said to Arc. The elves' shadows played across the water above Vahly's head. Light flashed through the waves, brighter than the sun, and she winced. They must have been securing Ryton with air magic, just in case he became a problem again.

Can you feel your earth magic? Arc asked her.

The ever-present drumming, the comforting pulse of the earth, tapped a rhythm in her blood. *It's there, but it's so weak. My ears are filled with the crashing waves of water magic.*

Perhaps you could cover your gills as the sea kynd have done in the past and come ashore? You might find your connection again outside the sea.

What did they use to do that?

Some sort of leaf. Let me ask the others.

While Arc questioned his kynd, his deep voice carrying through the water, Vahly turned to survey the expanse of ocean behind her. So far, none had followed. A few fish slithered between the currents, scales catching the light and shooting pain into Vahly's changed eyes.

Blinking, she turned her arm slowly, watching as the filtered sunlight glittered over her changed flesh. She swallowed bile.

What if she was forever changed? Gritting her teeth, she forced herself to stay put and wait on the elves' ideas.

After what felt like an eternity of being separated from Arc and the air and the earth, Arc called her name.

But she couldn't focus on him because an idea had bloomed inside her.

She was too separated from the land, from her home.

Bracing for the bright light and the raw air, she lunged over the rocks and sandy rise and leapt onto the grassy shore. Unable to breathe, blind as a newborn mountain cat, she dug her fingers into the ground.

The effect was immediate.

Her earth magic answered her silent, desperate plea, shaking under her knees and rising around her fingers and palms. The scent of turned land and green saplings and sap-filled branches flourished in the air as her body shook from head to toe.

Her scalp tingled. She shivered as a wave of warm magic grew from her fingertips, spreading like roots, driving the sea from her blood and her flesh and her heart. A blast of power coursed through her, pushing her to standing, an invisible hand of magic drying her and shifting her body into the one to which she'd been born.

A grin stretched Arc's handsome face and formed a dimple in each cheek. "She has returned to us." He knelt and bowed his head, his black hair falling like a dark curtain. "My queen."

Vahly studied her arms, her wrinkled clothing, her

human toes that were thankfully devoid of webbing. She breathed deep. Thank the Source. She was herself again.

Rigel bowed his head a fraction, and Haldus and Ursae left Ryton in his cage of light and followed suit.

Arc was still kneeling. She walked over to him, touched his broad shoulders, and bent to whisper in his ear.

"You should probably find that surcoat of yours or some suitable replacement, or I might just have to show my gratitude for the rescue in a way the others might not wish to witness."

His chuckle ruffled her hair. They stood as one and faced his kynd.

Rigel glanced from Arc to Vahly. Something stirred in his eyes, deep and troubled. The other two shifted on their feet.

"What is it?" Though most of her body focused on the magic's pull toward Kyril and the Lost Valley, the strange urge to step between the other elves and Arc surged through her.

"There has been a great tragedy, Arcturus." Rigel's chest rose high and fell as he breathed unevenly, his forehead wrinkling as he frowned and looked into the distance, toward the Forest of Illumahrah. "The Sea Queen struck our home."

Arc's cheeks lost their color, and Vahly gripped his hand. His fingers tightened around hers. "Cassiopeia?"

Haldus's mouth became a thin line, and Ursae closed her eyes.

Rigel met Arc's eyes. "Only a few ancient trees survive on the eastern boundary. But Arcturus...all are dead, save us."

Arc stumbled backward as if hit by a killing wave himself. Tears burned Vahly's eyes as she watched the pain of such a loss flood his features and drown the happiness that had been there just moments ago. She could still see regal and kind Cassiopeia at the elven crowning ceremony, the way Cassiopeia had touched Arc's cheek and smiled, how she'd greeted Vahly like kin.

All that peace and beauty. That entire ancient home. Gone.

Vahly too had lost her kynd. Astraea's ocean had devoured every last one of them and left her orphaned and alone. Though she knew the love of the Lapis and the Call Breakers, a place in her heart had always been and would always be left hollow and wanting.

An ache spread through Vahly's chest as Arc pulled her to him. He didn't make a sound. He only shuddered slightly and held on tightly. Vahly whispered to him, nonsense words that couldn't possibly help, but she said them anyway, lost at how to help him.

As Vahly let Arc hold her, the others gathered close to put hands on Arc's back and arm in support.

Vahly was already too late. She'd failed to save the elves. Who else would die while she was too weak to defeat the sea kynd? Would the Jades be next? The Call Breakers? The Lapis?

A darkness rose inside her, dampening the feel of the earth magic and smothering the sound of its drumming.

Arc stilled, then pulled back. The others released him and gave them a bit of space, their eyes red and their shoulders slumped with grief. Arc took Vahly's face in his large hands.

"No, you do not give up." His eyes flashed as he put a hand over her heart. "I can feel the sadness weakening you, drawing you down. But you are stronger than the darkness. You are the warrior who rages into the grief of life and fights for the joy, the beauty, the peace. Fight on, my queen. Fight on. We stand with you."

Vahly's heart beat hard under the weight of his words.

How many would be left standing with her at the end?

CHAPTER SEVENTEEN

Nix flew away from the Lapis palace, glad but feeling guilty as she left the cries of the dying and the rightfully fretting but still exhausting Kyril. His questions about Vahly's abduction and the rescue efforts—images in Nix's mind of Vahly's face and the elves—never ceased.

Wings sagging a bit, she landed outside the cider house and closed her eyes in relief to hear mugs clanking and the exchange of gold and precious stones. She was home. *Source, please help Vahly get home too.*

Nix walked through the front door and crossed her arms, surveying the gorgeous mess of gamblers, smugglers, and old friends. She smiled. "Call Breakers, we have some work to do."

Heads turned and a welcoming shout went up.

"Nix! Come here and let me welcome you home properly!"

"Oh, my finest dreams have become reality. Our matriarch is returned!"

Nix snorted though she was mightily pleased with the flattery. She sauntered through the main room, dragons stepping aside to let her through. She found Aitor and Euskal near the kitchen door, smoke streaming from their nostrils.

"Did I interrupt an entertaining argument? So sorry, lads." She patted Aitor's scarred face, and a lazy grin spread over his damaged mouth.

"It's nothing, Nix." Euskal blinked his shifty eyes. "How is Vahly doing?"

Nix saw no need to hold back information from her Call Breakers. She turned, spread her arms wide, and told them the story of their Earth Queen and what the sea kynd had accomplished.

"And so we must break into three groups. The first will remain here." She noticed Baww behind the bartop. "Baww, you will select those who stay to keep the cider house running. A second group, volunteers only, will go to the Lapis and help them with their sick."

"I heard they had some right awful plague," Baww said, an empty mug in his hand.

Nix nodded. "Indeed they do, and if you volunteer, I will reward you handsomely. But know this. You may become infected yourself. Granted, we are a strong bunch—"

"No leader, no leash!" they all called out in unison.

"So perhaps some of you will kindly risk it for our new allies in this war against the sea. A third group will come with me and see what we can do to help Queen Vahly in her escape. The elves might need defense if they must escape themselves or if they have Vahly and need to get onto land."

"I'd like to go with you," Aitor said, raising a hand.

"Of course," Nix replied before facing the room at large. "We will talk about this in one hour after I've had a bath. Drink on and think about where you'd like to help, my darling Call Breakers."

"To Nix!"

All raised their drinks.

"To Nix!"

As the drinking and discussions rose in volume, Nix looked at Euskal. "Will you come with me to aid our girl too? And Miren perhaps. Where is she, anyway?" The bald female was usually attached to Euskal's hip.

Euskal swallowed and looked out the side door. "Miren's sister died from the wounds she sustained during her battle with the sea kynd."

Nix knew Miren and her sister had been estranged ever since Miren had broken the Call with Amona. Miren's sister had been suffering from spelled salt water wounds for well over a month. Nix's blood boiled, thinking of how the sea kynd had given that female one of the longest and most painful deaths there was.

"Please give her my condolences. I would be honored to attend a ceremony if I haven't already missed it."

"It was three days ago." Euskal shook his head, then leaned in to whisper, "Miren isn't right in the head. Something about the death changed her. She seems... desperate. And she's been avoiding me."

Hmm. Nix would have someone tail Miren for a day

and see if anything was amiss and then report back to Baww while she was gone.

She took Euskal's chin between her thumb and forefinger and tipped his head toward hers. "Don't you worry. I will figure her out, and we will help her. She is one of us. Forever."

Euskal frowned and shifted his weight. "I don't know, Nix. I have a very bad feeling about what she's getting into."

"I'm sure I've dealt with worse, darling." Nix left him and headed upstairs for that bath, knowing that one of her Call Breakers would have filled and heated the tub the moment she'd arrived. Baths were a ritual for her, and she never missed one upon returning home after a job. But she was in a hurry now, and there would be no relaxing. She'd slept for a few hours at the Lapis palace, and now she was desperate to get back to Vahly, to find her, to aid in any way possible. This bath was not a luxury but a means to an end; it would help Nix fight and fly her best.

Upstairs, she hurried through her chamber's round doorway, her hand brushing the wrought iron red hat flowers that decorated the framing. Thankfully, no one was inside her bedroom. She needed peace, and her Breakers somehow sensed that. They truly were family. She crossed the carpeted floor and entered a side room where a bath steamed in the corner.

She disrobed and sank into the water, fully planning on visiting the edges of the fire marshes afterward to renew her energy before taking off with those who decided to join her.

But what if they flew to the western mountains and the elves hadn't found Vahly? What then?

Inhaling the scorchpepper leaves that some lovely soul had placed in the water, she tried to calm herself. It wouldn't do any good to panic.

After a sound scrubbing, Nix flew from her balcony, veering away from the flooded Lost Valley and toward the earthblood that flowed at the borders of the fire marshes.

The night sky showed off diamond stars and thin veils of cloud. The air had grown crisp with the change in season, and it was easy to see the ground below.

Someone was leaving through the back door of the cider house.

Nix focused. It was Euskal.

Remaining high in the midnight air that dried her wet hair, Nix watched as Euskal met someone in the last section of the cider house's orchards. Between the zigzagging rows of apple trees, he spoke to a dragon in full dragon form, one with no spikes. Miren.

Euskal's human form wings spread wide as he gestured with his hands. He was obviously angry or upset. Miren's wings remained resolutely tucked as her head dipped toward the ground. With the lack of light and the angle from which Nix watched, it was impossible to tell what Miren was doing. Then there was a blast of fire and Miren had shifted into her human form. Their voices rose, then fell as they looked toward the cider house. There were two bags at Miren's feet. She removed clothing from the first bag and dressed quickly as Nix hovered far above. Then Miren took up the second bag and started off, taking the roundabout way toward the Red Meadow and the Lapis palace.

What was she doing?

Euskal flung up his hands and stormed back into the cider house.

Nix flew off, her mind setting the puzzle pieces into place.

Miren was definitely up to something foul. Euskal was trying to talk her out of it, but she wasn't listening. But what was Miren doing exactly?

Well, whatever it was, Nix didn't have the time to find out. She could set another Breaker on Miren's trail as planned. Vahly was Nix's priority for now.

Nix descended quickly and reclined beside a particularly powerful earthblood vein, soaking in the heated magic that wafted from its glowing and sluggish depths. Her fire magic sparked inside her, dragonfire rising and ready to roast some sea kynd.

Oh, she hoped she had a chance to burn down that sea kynd male who'd taken Vahly. That would be a job she'd savor fully. She felt absolutely no guilt about it at all.

CHAPTER EIGHTEEN

Amona, Vahly called out with her mind. *Mother? Can you hear me?*

Kyril? Please let me know you hear me.

Nix? I'm alive. I'm on the northwestern coast with Arc. We're heading toward the Lost Valley.

But there was no answer. Not from anyone. What would she find at the Lost Valley?

Vahly's hand went to where her sword normally hung from her belt. But, of course, her sword was gone, thrown into the ocean's deep by her enemies. She closed her eyes, feeling incredibly tired.

"Arc, none of them are speaking to me. Amona, Nix, Kyril. They're all silent."

Haldus looked east. "We met with Mistress Nix and your gryphon Kyril. They were kind to us and searched for survivors until we assured them none lived. They flew toward the Lapis palace to meet with Matriarch Amona and inform her of your capture."

A sad smile tugged at Vahly's mouth. She and Arc

traded a look loaded with fear and admiration for their friends. While they were escaping the sea kynd, Nix and Kyril had been looking after things here, aiding kin and doing their best to get help.

"They told us about the day you were taken, Earth Queen," Rigel said, "and how Arcturus dove in after you. We guessed all were headed to Tidehame." His gaze touched Arc's forehead. "I know we are mourning, but there is the business of the elven crown."

Arc's eyebrows drew together, then his face cleared and he sighed, grief like a heavy cloak on his shoulders. "I am next in line."

Ursae clasped her pale hands and blinked up at him. "Will you take the crown and continue our legacy as best we can in this state?"

Arc cocked his head. "Was that a marriage proposal, Ursae?"

Heat roared through Vahly's cheeks, and she fisted her hands. She wanted to demand the elven girl back away from Arc, but this was Arc's decision to make. It was one thing for Arc to consider Vahly as a mate when all was well with his kynd, but now…

Ursae bowed her head to Arc. "If you wish it, I am willing. For our kynd." She looked up, her gaze stroking his face. "I have always admired you."

It was all Vahly could do not to cut that elf down right then and there. Gritting her teeth, she spun and walked toward Ryton so she wouldn't say something ridiculous.

At the sight of Ryton bleeding and slumped inside yet another magical cage, all her jealousy over Arc and Ursae faded. She knelt and reached a hand through the lines of light. His skin was like hers had been, tough and glimmering.

"Thank you for rescuing me. I'm still your enemy. I'm no fool. But you saved me when you could've left me for dead. I will see that they heal you and return you to the sea. Eventually." They couldn't simply plop him back into the water. He'd be killing dragons and working for the Sea Queen again in no time.

"You may as well kill me," Ryton said, his voice raw and splintered. "She will when you release me into the water. I think I'd prefer your version of death to hers."

Vahly stood and crossed her arms, doing her best not to hear Arc's conversation with the other elves, a discussion about lines of hereditary power and breeding that was only going to make her sick with jealousy.

"Your queen is a real treat, that's for sure," Vahly said to Ryton as he squinted in the bright sunlight passing through his air magic cage.

"She isn't known for her kindness."

"No, she sure isn't. Why did you save me? Or better yet, why did you work for someone you think so little of? Or even better than that, what is that thing on your back?"

Ryton's head lolled to the side. He took a disjointed breath and raised himself onto an elbow. "You remind me of my younger sister, Selene." He glanced at Vahly's wind-tossed hair.

"She must be worried about you."

"She is dead."

Oh. Well, he wasn't getting too much sympathy here. Vahly had lost loved ones too, at the hands of Ryton and his kynd. "Was she slaughtering elven children at the time? Or was that during one of your kynd's many sneak attacks on the Jades?"

Ryton's throat moved in a swallow. "We were fighting your dragons. The Lapis. The matriarch burned her to death."

Vahly's hands loosened, and she stared. Amona had killed this male's sister. Vahly had seen Amona kill many, but to know who the warrior had been… This felt different.

"Selene's most dominant trait was her curiosity. She longed to learn about every type of creature in the world. In water and on land. She didn't care that showing such enthusiasm for dragon ceremonies and human art was unacceptable to our kynd, taboo even. She read and read, and she pushed me to bring back items from human shipwrecks and ruins. The day she died, it was her first mission. I begged her to stay back, away from the front lines, but she was dauntless, and I couldn't hold her back. She was fighting that day, so I know why Matriarch Amona killed her. That's the first time I've admitted that fact. Warriors die, and my sister was a warrior. I will never forgive the dragon queen, but I do understand her acts. They fight for their own as we fight for our own."

Vahly's shirt felt too tight, the sun too hot. She spun to see the elves still in deep debate, Arc in his thinking pose with one arm tucked under the other. He tapped his lip with his thumb and squinted, speaking quickly in elvish.

"Will you heal him at some point tonight?" Vahly said to the elves. "I can't stand to see any more torture today. Keep an eye on him though."

Ryton sat up, crossing his legs. His trousers were still soaked. "I won't attack you or the others here."

"The promise of a sea kynd." Vahly snorted. She opened her lips, ready to regale him with all those she'd lost due to his kynd, but Arc's gentle voice stopped her.

"I will heal him soon," Arc said. "But first, Rigel wishes to crown me so that my magic will grow stronger for the fight to come."

He looked every inch the Elven King. His gaze was black and unwavering. Haldus, working a sparkling spell on the bag he carried, had provided Arc with an emerald cloak and a dark shirt. Arc stood tall, the cloak snapping in the wind, the thick cloth like dark wings around him. Magic curled around his fingers and temples, spinning more quickly as if it knew the gravity of the situation.

"That makes sense. I hate that it's under such a pall, but Cassiopeia would want you to take the reins of your people, to help them survive this."

Arc took her hand, a question in his eyes. Oh, the pain he must be in. She couldn't imagine it. She'd lost her kynd when she was still a babe in arms. She had no idea how it would feel to get such news now.

Swallowing, she brushed her palm along his forearm. "Do as you see fit for your kynd, and together we will fight and win against the sea."

He smiled, relief relaxing the wrinkle between his black eyebrows. "Thank you." Leaning in, he dragged his lips lightly over her cheek, then her ear. Shivers danced down Vahly's neck as he whispered, "But you'll always be my queen."

Ursae glared at Vahly but dipped her head respectfully as Arc turned to speak. "I accept the role of Elven King." He took a knee in front of Rigel.

Rigel held out both hands, his fingers hovering near Arc's temples. "May the Source bless your power and your heart. May the Blackwater rise in your blood and beat back any bent leanings. May you reign for one thousand years."

A shout erupted in Vahly's head, distant but urgent.

My girl! You live! There were tears in Nix's telepathic voice. *I am on my way north to help!*

Vahly put a hand over her roiling stomach, so glad to hear Nix, but also cold with fear at what she needed to tell her. *You can go back. We have a plan.*

Vahly, we are with the Lapis, and there is bad news.

I know about Illumahrah, Vahly said. *I'm with Arc, Rigel, and the rest.*

It's not that, Vahl. It's the Lapis. Do you remember the plague that hit the sea kynd a long time ago? When their finned bodies washed ashore in scores, their flesh cloaked in violet sores?

Vahly's gaze snapped to Arc. He was by her side in a blink, his new crown of churning magic swirling about his head.

Vahl, three score of the dragons here are infected. Already, fifty-two are dead. I fear you shouldn't come. You could catch this plague. But I know you, and you won't listen, and you'll want to see Amona and Helena and that little Ruda.

Are they sick too? Vahly gripped Arc's cloak, desperate to hear a *no.*

Amona doesn't look herself, but no, she hasn't taken sick yet. Helena and Ruda are rushing around here like fruit bats after a summer storm. They are well enough.

Kyril? Longing threatened to sweep Vahly's legs and throw her to the ground. She missed Nix's wry smile, the sage and sandalwood scent of Amona's embrace, and the warm and steadying connection to Kyril more than she could put into words. *Can you tell him to speak to me, in his way?*

I don't think he can manage it, or he already would have. He is truly struggling with all of this death. I can't get him to talk to me either.

Vahly winced, almost feeling Kyril's pain. Absently, she rubbed her fingers and thumb together, imagining the silken feel of his wings. She inhaled, wishing his sweet animal scent would rise into the air. *We're coming. The elves will help us move quickly. I'm far. Near the Jade palace. I'm going to ask them for help.*

You'll probably have to do more than ask, Nix said. *Put that oath they swore to use. I wish I could be there to see Eux's face when you do. Source, I'm glad you're alive.*

The old Nix never would've been all right with Vahly asking the Jades for help. But after all they'd been through, petty clan loyalties didn't feel as important as banding together as one, all land creatures fighting for the same cause.

To stay alive.

CHAPTER NINETEEN

In the courtyard of Álikos Castle, amid yellow veil fish and towering, emerald coral, Queen Astraea forced a smile and adjusted her crown as her guards approached.

"He…General Ryton is gone. We lost him, my queen." The fool bowed low, his blue-brown hair tangled and dirty. Most likely from chasing Ryton, that elf, and the human.

How had they escaped? Venu's entire unit had been after them. "What exactly happened?"

The second guard was shaking. "They disappeared. They were there, the elf, the human, and General Ryton, and then they weren't. We even searched Scar Chasm, my queen. Nothing."

Air magic. It had to have been the elf's doing.

Astraea's lips pinched, but she found her smile again. She waved a hand and whirled around, swimming toward Álikos Castle, aiming for her chamber where she could shed this smile, then rage. "Of course you didn't find them. It's all part of my plan."

The guards stammered and whispered to five more soldiers who'd just arrived. "Of course," they said too loudly, their fear and confusion giving Astraea the worst headache.

"Be gone. I want to be alone."

She swam past the gate guards and those at her inner chambers, wishing for once that everyone wasn't at her beck and call or at least that they could give her a minimum of privacy. Throwing her doors open, she raged into the room and cut off Larisa's quiet melody.

"Shut the doors, singer. Then make me something. Strong." Astraea pressed her webbed toes into the floor, muttering and stomping across the private chamber under the glowing nautili, her blood bubbling like an earthblood vent. She threw her spear into the corner. "Think they can outsmart me, do they? They are much mistaken. When I get my hands on them—"

Larisa, flushed and trembling, handed over a net of fermented tideberries. "My queen."

Astraea ripped them from Larisa's hand and tore into the pungent fruit. The acrid taste matched her mood perfectly. She discarded the empty net and took a deep breath. Destroying her own chambers with angry spellwork wouldn't fix this. Astraea collapsed onto her couch.

"Larisa, sing to me. Sing to me before I lose my mind and take the entire sea with me."

The singer spun, her grin luminescent before she opened her mouth. The tune began deep and petal-soft, then developed a complex melody. It seemed like magic that one voice could make such music. The female was truly talented. Astraea lay back and closed her eyes.

When the song ended, she spoke quietly, her anger buried for now. "Larisa, that was marvelous. I made such a perfect choice in bringing you here. You help me think. I don't know how I ran the ocean before you."

Larisa's delighted murmurs were interrupted by a knock at the door.

"Get that, if you will, my darling masterpiece," Astraea said. "I need to rest. Tell them to be gone."

Larisa's voice combined with that of a male Astraea recognized as one of her door guards.

Astraea's mind returned to Ryton, the Earth Queen, and the elf. Ryton was in league with them. But when had he changed sides? When had his betrayal started and why? What was his motivation? It made no sense. She'd never admit it to a living soul, but the betrayal stung like a sea stinger's tail. She'd thought Ryton was true and wholly hers in every way.

Larisa touched Astraea's arm, making the queen startle. "What is it?" Astraea snapped.

The singer held out a package wrapped in sealinen. "The guard said someone brought this gift to you." Larisa grinned. "The folk love their queen."

A genuine smile found its way to Astraea's lips. "Indeed." She sat up and unfolded the package, the sealinen smooth between her fingers, the object inside weighty on her lap.

It was a carving of two men. She looked closer.

Ryton and Grystark.

"Who gave this to my guard?" Astraea was on her feet, swimming toward the door, veins throbbing in her temples.

This was no gift. This was a threat. Ryton had betrayed

her because someone had told him about Grystark's death. It didn't take a genius to untangle this message.

"Who was it?" she demanded as Larisa hurried to catch up.

"I don't know, my queen. They didn't say," Larisa kicked her slender feet to move more quickly. The azure fins on her fingers trembled as she opened the doors for Astraea.

The guards spun to stand at attention, bubbles rising from their spears and into the glowing seaweed that grew from the ceiling.

Astraea shoved the nearest guard, making his gills flare in alarm. "Who gave you this?" She shook the sealinen and the carving, then whirled to face the second male. "Did you see the one who brought this to me? Do you even know how to do your job or should I feed you to the sharks so you're less of a wasted weight of flesh?"

"We didn't see who brought the package, my queen," the first guard said quickly.

The second guard shook his head. "The gift was left here."

Astraea advanced on him. "And you were blinded somehow?" She gripped one of his gills and pulled it back, making him wince and shake. "Why did no one see who brought this?"

"I don't know," the first guard said behind her. "Maybe during our shift switch, we missed it because Ajax had to grab a new spear and—"

"Buffoons!" Astraea turned away from the idiots and looked at Larisa. "I trust you. Can you have someone fetch the Watcher? I need her visions. Tonight."

Dashing into her chambers, she spoke a spell to slam her doors.

She would get her answers. And whoever sent this would die.

CHAPTER TWENTY

Ryton stared up at his captors. His head felt full of seaweed, and every breath was fresh torture. But now that the deed was done, now that he'd betrayed his queen, his heart was…

It was twisted.

Grystark would've done the same as Ryton. There was no way Gry would've let Astraea treat this young human the way she had. No matter what the human had done. It had been too cruel.

Right? Ryton wanted so badly to believe it.

And Gry would've killed Astraea for sending the army into that tunnel to die if he hadn't been struck down himself. Death during war was one thing, but dying for the tyrant they followed, no, he wouldn't have agreed to that, not when he left a grieving Lilia.

Ryton gripped the rough growth that sprouted from the ground, his knuckles going white and his jaw aching. He'd been tortured at the hand of his queen. He'd lost his only friend.

Sadness welled up through his chest, spilling over his ribs and pulling him to the earth again. He lay there, defeated in every way one could be beaten. All was lost to him. Nothing mattered. He had stopped one creature's torture only to throw his entire kynd into jeopardy.

The elves, all looking wan save the tallest, the one they were now calling king, approached Ryton's new cage of golden threads.

"I am Arcturus." The Elven King's voice rumbled like distant thunder, and magic hummed around him, violet and golden swirls of air magic that put Ryton on edge. This creature was in his element. Ryton, of course, was far from it. They could kill him so easily, so quickly. "I know we have been enemies in the past, but the Earth Queen tells me you made her rescue possible. I am endlessly grateful, although I'm guessing you don't care about my thanks."

The Earth Queen—they called her Vahly—leaned forward and stared into Ryton's eyes. She smelled strongly of ancient power, a counter to Astraea's scent and foul to his gills. "Thank you, General Ryton. I don't understand why you did what you did, but truly, thank you. Now, we have a little problem. I'm sure you'd like to return to your realm, but we can't release you to fight us again. We are left with the problem of what to do with you."

"Just kill me." Ryton took a wheezing breath, the beast on his upper back clicking its pincers. "This thing will do it anyway, in its time. And I think I'd rather not wait for that experience."

Vahly pursed her lips and raised both of her light eyebrows. "Don't blame you. But..." She looked to Arcturus, who tilted his head and held out a hand toward

Ryton. They seemed to have some sort of unspoken communication. "We can't kill you." She stood, brushing off her trousers and then starting to braid her hair.

"Agreed," Arcturus said, waving the other elves over. They reached into the air magic cage and touched Ryton's wounds.

Ryton froze as they whispered in elvish and a warmth traveled up his legs, into his torso, along his arms, and over his head. A wave of relief crashed over him, and he stretched out on the smelly ground as the magic barriers disappeared.

The silver-haired elf, Rigel, perhaps, snagged Ryton's dagger. Ryton wore no other weapons they needed to worry about. His spear was long gone. Ryton winced. Who was he now without Gry, without Astraea, without his magic?

Dragging himself to standing, he held out his hands. "If you're going to keep me alive, then will you listen to my thoughts about our kynds and this world?"

Vahly was already walking up a winding path. She waved at everyone to move on. "Fine. But we have to get to the Jade palace and find some dragons to carry us to the Lapis quickly. Before your queen comes for us again."

Ryton struggled to keep up with the elves. The female, Ursae, followed him, nudging his steps with blasts of air magic that made it easier for him to walk quickly. The magic felt like a strong current sweeping underfoot. It was unsettling, to say the least.

He cleared his throat. He would bare all. Just give them his truth. He had no more energy or will for deceit or strategy. Not now with Gry's death still punching his chest every other heartbeat. "Astraea will be incensed when she realizes both you and I are gone. She will strike again, and it's a solid guess that she'll go for your Lapis."

Vahly glanced over her shoulder. "She questioned me about where Matriarch Amona sleeps in the palace." The Earth Queen's lip curled. "Of course, I lied, but I don't think Astraea expected the truth. She wanted to frighten me. It was only more torture."

"But I beg of you," Ryton said, his throat burning, "to consider the way in which you fight the sea. I want to hate you, Earth Queen, but I can't seem to manage it."

Arcturus chuckled, though the sound still held the gravity of grief. He had to be low knowing that his kynd was all but gone. Ryton shuddered. The sea kynd could lose this war, and then Ryton would know the feeling too, if the evil thing on his back let him live to see it.

"What I mean is, not all of the sea kynd are as foul as you might believe." Nausea pushed against Ryton's senses, and he had to stop and struggle through three full breaths before they could continue. This wretched place. How were they comfortable here? It seemed impossible. He swallowed roughly and continued, Lilia and the scout Echo specifically on his mind, "I thought all of land kynd were foul. But I was wrong. I ask only that if there comes a point in the battles ahead in which you can somehow spare a portion of the ocean for my kynd, please consider it. There is a female. The widow…is that the correct word for a grieving mate?"

"Yes," Ursae croaked out behind him.

Rigel spun and glared. "Ursae. King Mattin was not your mate."

The female elf raised her pointed chin. "Not in name but

in deed. I know he was bent, but I loved him, and he loved me."

"He used you," Rigel snapped. "Canopus—"

Arcturus held out a hand. "She knows her own business, Rigel. Let it go."

Ryton's stomach lurched, and he vomited into the dry dirt. If they didn't kill him, this place would do the job well enough. With no more energy for talking, he walked in silence until the sun blessedly diminished in power and the cored hillside that had to be the Jade dragon palace emerged from a row of jagged, gray trees.

It was mind-blowing that he was here, walking into the heart of his kynd's most feared enemy. Perhaps the Jades weren't as crafty as the vile Lapis, and Ryton didn't hold exactly the same hatred toward Matriarch Eux as he did Matriarch Amona, but the Jade palace remained horrifying. He was out of his element. Weakened by the black beast's magic that used to make him stronger. Would the Jades even listen to Vahly long enough to hear why Ryton was there and not bleeding out on the ground? Jades struck first and asked questions later.

But there was little he could do about it. He had to follow Vahly into the dark and pitted cave they called a palace, or else the elf at his back would kill him immediately, before he'd had time to figure out what his new plan needed to be and what he had to live for. He wanted that time, he realized belatedly. He wasn't yet ready to give up on life.

But he doubted the Jades cared much for his inner philosophical debate.

Matriarch Eux would most likely burn him alive on sight.

CHAPTER TWENTY-ONE

"Halt!" Two Jade guards in their humanlike forms flew over the palace entrance's three sets of narrow stairs and barred Vahly and the rest with drawn swords.

Not so long ago, she would've quaked in her boots at these two. Now as she stood in bare feet, in contact with the earth and her magical birthright echoing through her blood, the guards seemed like wolf pups. They could bite, but they weren't much of a threat if their parent wasn't nearby.

"I am your Earth Queen, and you swore allegiance to me. Now move your green tails before I pull this mountain down on your heads or your matriarch hears about this infraction and fries you both for her supper."

The guards growled, but they flew from the steps and allowed the party to pass.

"Nicely done," Arc whispered, his voice teasing but still heavy with grief. She'd seen warriors like him set sadness aside like they were taking off a pair of boots for the night. It seemed Arc too had this skill.

"Thank you," she said. "I think I could get used to this whole queen thing. How do you feel about being a king?"

His magic curled around his head, his crown luminous against the sun setting beyond the palace stairs and the far-off northern mountain range.

"I feel more like your equal now, and I can't say I don't enjoy that sensation."

She smiled, wanting to keep joking but afraid to hurt him by saying the wrong thing.

The palace entrance's ceiling disappeared into the dark, the lower reaches lit by large beeswax candles that smelled of honey and wildflowers.

"That, I did not expect," Vahly said, gesturing to the nearest flame.

Arc lifted an eyebrow as he adjusted his cloak, his movements slower than what was normal for him. "I would've guessed they'd use the bodies of their enemies to light their hallways."

"Yes, exactly."

He almost laughed, but it seemed as though the shadows of those they had lost tore the smile from his lips. Vahly understood. He would need time to move forward after the loss of so many friends and family. He might not be able to truly laugh for a long, long time.

Heart aching for him, Vahly reached for his hand, then quickly brushed his palm with her fingertips before pulling away. He glanced at her, eyes sincere and unblinking.

It's so much to bear.

The candles' light appeared to soak into his skin and bones, making him luminescent. As the Elven King, he was the embodiment of the oldest power on this island. The dark color of his eyes—like pools of Blackwater—drew Vahly closer. Arc was so many things to her now. Friend. Ally. Confidant. The one she looked for first upon waking.

She didn't say anything back. She just took his hand again, this time gripping tightly, pouring some of her strength into him.

They walked on, the candlelight pooling on the palace corridor's floor. Soon, they reached a guarded arch that led into a massive space with a dais and a throne of jade. The guards let them pass, and Vahly guessed they'd been informed telepathically to allow the party access to Matriarch Eux's throne room. The chamber smelled metallic, like blood had been recently spilled, and, indeed, a darkened stain marred the smooth, stone floor. The Jades were known for their brutal competitions of strength and battle prowess. Perhaps they held such entertainments here for their matriarch.

But where was Eux? Where was her court? Normally, it seemed as though that nightmare of a dragon, Zarux, was always around when Vahly had dealings with the Jades.

Ryton looked around, face drawn with worry and the weakness that his cursed burden seemed to inflict on him. Arc whispered something in elvish to Rigel, Haldus, and Ursae.

Suddenly, Vahly's skin prickled, and a wind coursed from the darkened recesses of the space above.

The elves and General Ryton gasped.

Matriarch Eux descended in her human form, smoke curling from her nostrils and mouth and a glint of fury in her bright orange eyes. "Welcome, Earth Queen."

The scales around Eux's face and along her arms were

decorated in jade links that held the teeth of lost loved ones. The matriarch dipped her head and Vahly mimicked the gesture, pulse knocking her teeth around. Well, at least the guards hadn't shaken Vahly. Perhaps someday she'd be likewise immune to a matriarch's dangerous presence.

Tapping claws against a large ruby set in the sheath of her short sword, Eux looked from Vahly to Arc.

"And greetings to you, Elven King. This is a new development." She gestured to his crown of dark and light.

Arc winced like she'd struck him. "The Forest of Illumahrah has experienced a terrible tragedy. The Sea Queen flooded our plateau and killed all but us. I have taken the heavy mantle of leadership for what is left of my kynd."

"You seem powerful. That will help. It's too bad we've lost so many of your kynd before we even had the chance to work together against the sea folk."

Vahly stepped forward, anger itching under her skin. "It is a personal tragedy. Not merely a strategic loss."

Eux waved a hand. "Of course. Of course. Now…"

Something had distracted her.

"I have been in the western region, securing my familiar," Vahly said. "Now we need help to travel quickly to the Lapis lands. We ask for your assistance."

But Eux didn't seem to be listening. Her nostrils flared, snakeskin green, and her eyes widened then narrowed. She pushed past them to stand over Ryton.

"What is this?" she demanded, her voice like lightning.

Black plumes of smoke slithered from her nose and gathered like clouds. The scent of dragonfire, citrus and charcoal, suffused the air.

She was going to light him on fire.

"Matriarch Eux, please hear us out."

To his credit, Ryton didn't bend or bow, just stared into her eyes.

"How does he breathe here?" Eux slashed a talon toward Ryton's shoulder, aiming for the black beast's arm. Blood welled where Ryton's skin met the thing's bone-like appendage. "What foul trick is this?"

Arc glanced at Vahly, silently asking if she wished for him to attempt an explanation, but keeping Ryton alive had been her choice and she had to do the persuading.

She stepped between Ryton and Eux, smoke choking her and forcing her to take shallow breaths. "During my time searching the sunken Bihotzetik ruins, he took me into the sea. He deserves to die, surely, but he changed his mind and all but sacrificed himself to create an opportunity for me to escape. He is the reason I'm not currently strung up dead across a coral cross fashioned by Queen Astraea."

Eux blinked. "But why?"

"She reminded me of my sister, Selene." Ryton rubbed a hand over his beard. "Scoff if you wish. Kill me if it suits you. But know that I will never again do her harm. I find my hands are unwilling to be the death of this human female."

"Well, isn't that touching." Eux snorted and began circling Ryton. Then she whirled and faced Vahly.

Vahly flinched but stood her ground as the matriarch opened her mouth to speak.

"Amona knew about your journey into Bihotzetik's flooded ruins, didn't she? You two decided this without informing me. You thought it would be just fine to risk yourself, our only chance at defeating Astraea, by plunging right into enemy territory like a complete fool because of some twinge of newly born magic stirring inside you?"

Lifting her head, she blew dragonfire above them, temporarily blinding everyone with the sudden brightness.

Vahly's mind sprinted through explanations. But Eux had called Vahly their *only chance*, so perhaps no excuses needed to be given. Maybe Eux would bend to Vahly's wishes if Vahly acted more like a Jade and owned her place in this world.

Matching Eux's glare, Vahly raised her voice. "Matriarch Eux, I don't need to detail my decisions as Earth Queen to you. You swore your allegiance, as did your fellow dragons. If you choose to question me and attempt to intimidate me, you're only hindering your own survival, both by lengthening my journey to end this war and by tempting the bonds of your oath to me. So if you are finished with your pointless growling, I suggest you find dragons enough to carry us to the Lapis palace so I can continue trying to save your ungrateful scales!"

Eux's eyes glittered, and Vahly felt like a ram about to be devoured. But a smile spread over the matriarch's emerald face. "Much better, Earth Queen," she said, her voice crackling as if sparks hid between the syllables. "It pleases me that you have at last found the fire inside you, the fire that will deliver my kynd."

Arc looked at Vahly from the corner of his eye, grinning and coughing to cover a surprised chuckle.

Eux stepped away and spoke to two females who stood by the door.

Vahly looked back at the elves and exhaled in silent but dramatic relief, making them all smile despite their pain.

Soon they were ushered into a collection of rooms on the next floor up, given rough but hearty fare, and told to wait while the Jades gathered supplies for the ailing Lapis.

Magic drumming inside her, pushing her to run the entire length of the island, climb Kyril's furred back, and fly with all haste possible to the Lost Valley, Vahly walked into Arc's chamber. Fatigue rode her shoulders like Ryton's beast did his, but she wanted to help Arc, to be there for him as he worked on opening up the reality of his loss.

Source, give me strength.

Beside a small fire, he sat on a rug that showed the Jade's symbol, a dragon skull. He was sharpening his throwing knives, but as she approached, he looked up, pausing in his work.

His gaze met hers, and heat snapped between them.

He dropped the knives, closed the distance between them, and took her into his arms.

CHAPTER TWENTY-TWO

Vahly's breath caught in her throat as Arc's hands swept up her neck to cradle her face. His eyes glittered with unshed tears. "Vahly, I..." His throat moved, and he looked away.

She pressed her forehead to his, soaking in his warmth. "I'm so sorry for what you've lost."

He turned his head, his cheek against her forehead. He started to speak, but a sob choked him.

Tears flowed freely from Vahly's eyes, her chest exploding with the pain she felt for him. She felt as though they were both falling into the sea, cold waves of isolation sweeping them under, dragging them deep.

Vahly gripped him, holding on as if her life depended on it, the entirety of what she'd gone through under the sea and what they'd missed here on land threatening to drown her more assuredly than any sea ever could. "Cassiopeia would be so proud to see you now, carrying on."

"My home," he said, voice hitching. "I have to be strong, and, Vahly, I'm not sure I can do it."

"Don't be strong right now, love. Just weep."

He sagged against her, head on her shoulder and hands tight on her sides as grief washed over him.

She whispered into his pointed ear, wondering how they'd ever been unaware of the other's existence. This felt more real to her than anything else.

The year Vahly became a woman, she'd felt the loss of human kynd like it had been a fresh grief. Amona hadn't given her platitudes and positive plans. She'd encouraged Vahly to imagine all the things she was missing without her family and her kynd. Tears had flowed, hard and ugly, that day. But bleeding the sadness out had led to a healing of sorts. She'd never be truly whole, but that openness, that release, had made it possible for her to function again, to find her footing in this world. She wanted that for Arc. He deserved it and more. So much more.

"Let it flow out of you. Tell me what you will miss."

He pressed his forehead to hers again, his lips parted. "The joy. We were one. I don't know who I am without them. Who am I, Vahly? Who am I?"

Vahly took his face in her hands. "You are Arcturus. Alchemist. Warrior. Dearest friend." It most likely wasn't what he wanted, but the words were all she could find. Stones, she wished she were wiser. "You lead Haldus the stout, Rigel the wise, and Ursae the prodigal. That is not nothing, Arcturus of the royal house of Illumahrah. It is a high calling indeed, and you will fight by my side and help me save our kynds from the evil designs of those who wish only to destroy." Chills raked Vahly's arms. She knew there would be more loss, more grieving, before all this was done. And Arc was no fool. He knew this too. "Together, we will do this. As you said to me, we will fight for the joy, the beauty, and the peace. We will find it again. Together."

His fingers cupped her chin, and he drew her mouth to his. His lips were soft and salted with tears, and she thought her heart would burst with love for him. Kissing her deeply, gentle but firm, he held on to Vahly like she was his only solace, pulling her to him, his body strong against hers. His magic coursed through the room, a breeze stirring the velvet curtains on the bed, tugging at the tasseled ends of the rug, and buffeting the fire into a snapping blaze. He brushed his thumbs across her jawline and kissed his way down her throat. Tingling sparks danced down the length of her, and she gasped, joy blending with the heartache, bittersweet and aching.

She pulled away from him, took his hand, and led him to the rug by the fire, wanting the light and the warmth. Lying down, side by side, his stomach to her back, they watched the reaching flames and whispered comfort to one another until the rose hue of sunrise streamed through the carved window.

CHAPTER TWENTY-THREE

The Jades didn't complain about Vahly and the elves asking to ride their backs. Not even the dragon tasked with carrying Ryton. As Arc had done on Nix, Vahly slid between the two primarily crystalline spikes at the base of Yarun's neck. He was one of Eux's personal guards and was built low to the ground and had lean muscle running through him that tensed as Vahly adjusted her position. More than anything, the lack of grumbling Jades spoke to the immediacy of the Sea Queen's threat.

As they took off in a sweeping circle, the coastline shimmered in the distance. Matriarch Eux had shown Vahly the territory the sea had already risen to flood. The Jades had lost a third of their lands. Four bald mountain peaks rose from the waves, and it wasn't difficult to imagine the horrible story those places told. A single tree, broken and leafless, sagged in the ocean wind. With a strong wave like the one Astraea had used to kill the elves, the Jade territory would be completely submerged.

The reason Eux's throne room had been empty was because most of the Jades had been off building up land breaks to ensure the lapping waves came no further. What little good it would do. But Vahly understood why a leader would want to keep her folk busy at such a time.

Vahly felt like she was betraying Kyril by riding Yarun. The Jade's flying was far smoother, but Kyril hadn't been flying for nearly as long. Wind crashed over Yarun's sage-colored head and around his mossy-hued spikes before brushing through Vahly's hair and whipping her mended and washed shirt against her arms and throat. The Jades had given her a new leather vest, too, easy enough for them to fashion in a night with their quick and crafty talons, properly sized for such work when they were in their human form. The Jades' leanings toward craftwork and textile creation had surprised Vahly and the elves. During the time before she'd gone to Arc's chamber, she'd seen several rooms of Jades in human form, stitching, weaving, and cutting fabrics in a rainbow of hues. Vahly smiled, thinking of how the vicious, ruthless Jades, even those in their prime, shared interests with the elder dragons of the Lapis clan.

The early morning bright blue of the sky gave way to an afternoon rainstorm, and Vahly watched in envy as the elves shaped golden spheres around themselves that seemed to keep off some of the rain. She had no such ability and was soaked by the time they landed for a meal and some rest.

Ryton dismounted from his dragon. With the water running over his face, he looked more like he had appeared under the sea—skin glimmering, pupils wide. He seemed to breathe easier in the rain shower, but his appearance threw a shiver down Vahly's back. Her magic thumped against her ribs. Why did the Source insist that she keep him alive? Sure, he'd saved her, but wasn't he still a threat? This seemed like lunacy. He could cut them all down in their sleep.

The rain slackened to a mist as Arc walked over, the scent of him like a balm.

Vahly looked up into his face and raised an eyebrow. "That little rain shield seemed comfortable."

Arc's lips tilted. "May I?" He lifted his palms, indicating that he could dry her with his air magic if she wanted.

"Pretty please with a long night of sleep on top." Valy stepped closer.

Tingling erupted over her scalp and down her limbs as his magic moved over her, hot and quick. Her breath came too fast, her chest rising and falling against his. Once the deed was done, he lowered his hands and pressed a kiss to her forehead. She inhaled the scent of resin and sun-warmed earth. His lips brushed down her temple and found her ear, where he nipped the top edge.

Vahly's body flamed, heat rising in her chest and stomach. "Trying to turn me into an elf? I wouldn't fight that. I think I'd look good with pointed ears."

His mouth moved just under her earlobe. "You would be beautiful as any kynd."

Vahly smiled, his words easing the ongoing pain of being separated from Kyril.

The Jades flew off to hunt for dinner as the sun slumped toward the last slice of sky. Rigel and Haldus brought Arc into an elvish conversation, Ursae standing outside their circle and looking ill.

After settling her bags against a boulder, Vahly decided to have a chat with Ryton.

He was sitting against a fallen oak, hitched up awkwardly to one side, the beast obviously causing discomfort.

"What do you think is going on now in your realm?" she asked, standing over him, wishing she still had her sword. She had her earth magic, but she hadn't trained an entire life with it like she had her blade. Stones, she missed that weapon and the comfort of its ivory hilt.

Ryton took a small bite of the root vegetables Haldus and Ursae had gathered just before the group had started their journey that morning.

"She will come after your heart, Earth Queen." Ryton's face held little emotion. "And mine as well. Lilia, though she thinks she is in a safe place, is as good as dead."

Vahly recalled the story of Grystark. "Lilia is the wife of your friend?"

He nodded. "She has kin in the far northern oceans. Beyond our usual trade and travel routes. She might be there. I didn't ask so I couldn't give up the information."

"There are sea kynd that far from your Blackwater source?" It was surprising they had chosen to settle such a distance from their access to the Source. Vahly had learned more about their underwater spring from Arc.

"As I argued earlier, many of our kynd are unlike what you are accustomed to encountering. Lilia's kin are peaceful. I beg you not to wipe them from the world without a thought."

"I don't think I can do that anyway."

"But if you eventually have the choice, the skill, will you stay your hand and consider them?"

Vahly didn't mind lying in card and dice games. Nor did she mind deceit when it worked to help her side in a fight. But here, seeing Ryton's sincere face, with the memory of the wounds he'd suffered for her fresh in her mind, she found she had no desire to be in the least bit dishonest about this.

"General Ryton, I can't make this promise. Not yet. My anger at your kynd runs through me like my magic. I would be lying if I made this promise to you. I still hate you and your folk for all that you have done. You stole my family. Every one of my nightmares as a child consisted of what your kynd did to my mother before she died. Was she ripped by ruthless teeth? Drowned, her lungs bursting near her heart? Did she call my name in the water even as your kynd tore her throat out, thoughtless of guilt or innocence? No, Ryton, I will not make any oaths to you. I despise this situation because I can see kindness in you. I see your valor and courage and goodness. But I'm not ready to swear anything to you. Maybe someday. But not now. And maybe never."

Guilt weighed on her as she left him, his gaze on her like a brand, burning against her back. But she wouldn't lie to him. It would be a betrayal that was beneath her. She would be his enemy to his face. At least she wouldn't act like that queen he had served for so long.

Not far from where Rigel, Haldus, and Ursae talked quietly, Arc was on one knee near a holm oak, touching the exposed parts of the tree's roots. He whispered something in elvish.

"What are you up to, elf?" she teased, trying to shrug off the weight of her conversation with Ryton. "Are you asking that tree to court you?"

He looked over his shoulder and smiled mischievously. "Are you jealous, Earth Queen?"

"I'm too tired to be jealous now, but I'm noting the feeling and will do my best to rile the emotion once I'm back to full strength."

"I look forward to the show." He stood and dusted his hands, his cloak brushing against the dormant red hat flowers and their delicate stalks. "If you must know, you nosey thing, I was speaking to the tree and asking it to form you a bed."

Vahly's mouth opened, and her hand went to her chest. "No."

"I was. I can see the fatigue in you, and it worries me. Though you have pain and worries enough to explain today's exhaustion, I believe it's because you need your familiar by your side. You could also use a good night's sleep."

Last night, dozing by the fire with Arc—it had been wonderful. But it was true that she hadn't slept much. She'd feared he would need her again, and she'd only closed her eyes for a few minutes here and there.

Arc stepped away from the oak. Waxy leaves grew from every possible spot along its branches. "Perhaps you should try to persuade this tree to extend itself for you. My ability to influence trees appears to remain limited to the trees of

Illumahrah." His gaze went to the southwest, where his destroyed home sat.

Not sure whether to say something comforting, Vahly stayed silent. Instead of speaking, she knelt at the foot of the tree and placed her right palm on the foremost root. Earth magic pounded through her flesh and flashed up her arm.

"Grow," she commanded.

Everyone had fallen silent. There was nothing. And then, a crack of wood…

The oak's roots rose like great snakes and slithered across the ground. Their girth expanded to four, five—ten times their original size before braiding themselves into a hammock of sorts.

Vahly smiled. "I guess that worked."

Ursae came up, her arms full of dry grass. "May I?" she asked Arc.

At his nod, she filled Vahly's new oaken bed, then covered the grass with her own cloak.

Vahly touched her arm. "Thank you, Ursae, but please, keep your cloak."

"I'm not cold. Take it. Please." The elf's light eyes studied Vahly's face. She seemed sincere enough.

"Thank you." Vahly watched her leave, wondering if Ursae's behavior spoke of acknowledged guilt or was a ploy to get into Vahly's good graces for some future goal.

Wind rose around them, and the branches of the oak waved wildly.

The Jades, in full dragon form, descended near Rigel and dropped two stags and a large doe. The dragons ate in their dragon form while Vahly and the elves roasted the dressed deer before sitting down to feast. Ryton's face twisted at the sight of the meat, and Vahly wondered what he had consumed under the sea. He pulled more root vegetables from the bag at his belt and chewed in silence.

What was Amona going to make of him? Vahly took a bite of warm venison, then swigged from her water skin. Would she threaten him like Eux had, or would she be curious?

Haldus broke into her thoughts. "Earth Queen, if you can fashion a bed, I would think you could also create an entire shelter for us."

She raised an eyebrow, thinking maybe he was asking a bit much from her considering her fatigue. She didn't care to entertain tonight. But perhaps his request spoke of his longing for his home, a place once filled with an oaken castle and homes magically formed from pines and beeches, moss and herb.

Setting her water skin and the rest of her meal on the ground, she spied another holm oak behind Haldus. All watched as she walked to the tree and pressed her hands against its trunk. She could almost feel the Jade dragons' gazes burning into her back. Their reluctance to change into their human forms during the journey troubled her. Vahly would've thought the Jades would want to discuss what had happened and what the plans were for their next move.

This larger oak cast a shadow over her, blocking out the sky's last turquoise and lemon light. She inhaled the tree's green scent as it vibrated under her hands. She was about to speak, to command the tree, but it ended up being unnecessary.

The tree exploded into a churning chaos of movement.

Dirt flew from the turned earth as roots and limbs and leaves swirled together and climbed over the camp. The ends of branches found one another to form a woven ceiling of oak.

Haldus's eyes twinkled as the tree saw fit to curl roots around each group—dragons, elves, and Ryton on his own, creating small, partially private chamber walls that sprouted leaves like it was springtime.

Heart beating excitedly, Vahly entered through the new structure's archway and found everyone peering from their respective chambers, faces pale with shock.

Arc was the first to speak. Grinning, he crossed his arms and leaned against the doorway into his new room. "Nix will be furious that she missed this."

A laugh bubbled from Vahly's throat. "I can already imagine her list of cider house improvements."

Vahly nestled into the bed she'd crafted first and pulled the cloak the Jades had provided over her to ward off the night's chill. With Ursae's cloak under her body and Arc in the chamber next door, she was quite comfortable.

They'd made it through the windy passes of the Jade territory, and the rest of the trip would go quickly. If Vahly's fears were on the mark, these would be the last nights of good rest for a long, long time.

CHAPTER TWENTY-FOUR

C hilly air scented with the aromas of the first signs of autumn, dying leaves, and fallow ground whipped across Vahly's face as Yarun and the other dragons soared toward the Lapis palace.

Almost to the palace, Mother, Vahly said to Amona.

Your welcome will be sparse, Daughter. Amona sounded intensely weary. Did she have the plague too? *Please do not think it is out of disrespect.*

Of course not. It's a long story, but I have one of the sea kynd.

She could almost feel Amona's shock and horror through their bond.

He rescued me from the Sea Queen, and my magic is telling me to keep him around. I know. It's madness. But I have to listen.

I don't think I can take him into our home, Amona said.

Then keep him caged outside the entrance. But we must keep him alive.

Driven by the increasingly intense prickling push of her magic, Vahly had urged the group to fly hard over the island, stopping only when the dragons absolutely needed a rest. Days of dust clogged the creases of her wrinkled clothing, and her stomach growled with hunger. Yarun hit the ground roughly, stumbling with fatigue and nearly throwing Vahly to the earth.

As she leapt down, clutching their bags, she noticed an iron cage set beside the entrance to the palace. Ryton's temporary home. Her stomach turned. She didn't like this situation. Not one bit.

Shaking off the unease, she faced Yarun. "Thank you."

The Jade shifted in a blast of white-orange flame, and she jumped back. Yarun's human form was similar to his dragon shape, lean and short. He had fierce eyes and a scar that ran the full length of his right side.

With a nod of respect, Yarun held a hand out for his bag, and Vahly tossed it to him before turning to follow Arc, Rigel, Haldus, and Ryton up the wide steps of the Lapis palace. The elves all had a touch of purple beneath their eyes, evidence of their grief and fatigue. Arc brushed dust from his cloak and hung back, matching step with Vahly.

She gave his arm a quick squeeze, then opened her mind to Kyril.

But it was unnecessary. The gryphon, much larger than Amona now, swooped onto the steps, lion claws digging into the worn stone like they were made of butter.

Vahly's heart danced as she reached him and pressed her face into the thick, golden fur on his front leg. He pulled away to dip his head submissively, but she yanked him back up, laughing. He nuzzled her with a huge but gentle beak, sending images into her mind—the sight of her landing on Yarun's back, her face flushed and grimy with the journey's dirt. She could feel Kyril's discomfort at her traveling with Yarun.

Don't worry. I prefer your flying by far, she said, hoping to comfort him.

And she truly must have because Kyril's presence soothed and empowered her, causing her magic to surge through her veins. She remained in contact with him, her fatigue fleeing away and her lingering injuries dissolving.

As two Lapis guards took a willing and weakened Ryton into the cage and two more escorted Rigel, Haldus, and Ursae inside, Arc joined Vahly. He ran a hand over the gryphon's tucked wing, smiling.

Kyril lowered his feathered head and remained there, showing submission until Arc touched his beak to release him.

"I blame you," a raspy voice said, "for all of my new wrinkles, queenie."

Nix sauntered down the stairs, and Vahly felt as though someone had lit a bright candle inside her heart. Nix was here and alive, and Vahly had at one time thought maybe they'd never speak again. She rushed to Nix and hugged her fiercely.

"Blackwater," Nix whispered, "I'm so happy you're still breathing. I thought I'd lost you, girl."

Nix's raspy breath tripped, and she held Vahly tighter. Nix's many rings pressed into Vahly's spine and side. Vahly laughed as Nix fluttered her wings to get them out of the way. Sighing, Vahly wished they could be at the cider house, running bets and teasing Dramour. She missed him so much. Ibai and Kemen too.

"That's quite enough now," Nix said, backing up and

wiping a tear. She blinked her yellow eyes at Arc. "You saved our Earth Queen." She took Arc's hand and patted it gently. "I am sorry for your loss. There are no words. Would you like for us to participate in a ceremony with you and the others?" Nix gestured to the scar on her palm. The night they'd mourned the ones Mattin had killed, they'd all offered a blood sacrifice in memory.

Arc touched Nix's shoulder. "I performed one with Rigel and the others already. But thank you very much for the offer."

"So you have taken up the crown?" Nix asked.

"I have." Arc's lips tightened into a line. "I had little choice."

Nix gave him a sad grin. "You make a fine Elven King, Arcturus. I have full faith in your ability to bring your kynd to strength again."

Arc bowed slightly to Nix.

The three of them climbed the steps and walked into the palace, Vahly bracing herself for the pain of seeing her family struck by illness.

The feasting hall had been turned into a hospital, the floors open to the earthblood vents to help the dragons heal. There had to be a hundred of them—old, young, and in-between—lying around in full dragon form on haphazard beds of velvet, large pieces of pyrite-lined and deep blue lapis lazuli, as well as mounds of shining coins and gold nuggets.

Vahly's throat closed. Their loved ones had brought their family treasure here to help them heal. She gripped Arc's arm and Kyril's fur, her hands shaking.

"So many," she whispered under the sound of groans

and the scrape of tails against the loot they'd gathered over millennia.

Nix took a pitcher of water from Euskal, the narrow-eyed Call Breaker that usually could be found next to bald Miren, having smoke ring blowing contests at the cider house. He carried two more jugs besides, scales mottled with fatigue but not plague, thankfully.

Refilling a cup for a plague-touched member of Lord Maur's retinue, a large fellow who Vahly thought was named Tuxi, Nix explained the progression of the plague.

"It began with this one's master."

"Lord Maur has it?" Vahly hated the dragon, but she didn't wish eroding scales and a painful death on him.

"He did. He passed yesterday."

Vahly's mouth hung open. He'd been such a huge presence in her life, and now he was dead. Just like that.

Nix continued. "Just after I arrived back here, he collapsed when I was dining with Amona and the rest of the Lapis. That's when Helena noticed the brittle edges of his scales. The next day his eyes went poppy red, and the following day he left this world. Soon, ten more had the plague, including Aitor."

Vahly's stomach turned. "No." Aitor was Nix's primary spy and a friend to them both. Scarred badly over his mouth and throat, he'd survived a wild battle between the Jades and the Lapis before he'd broken the Call and started working for Nix.

"Aitor is alive. He is actually in my bed at the cider house." She rolled her eyes. "He is quite enjoying the attention of nearly dying. It seems he will survive, although his ego may slaughter the rest of us. A few have survived this thing. All is not lost. It does feel that way at the moment."

A youngling, pale blue, slumped beside the doorway.

Vahly knelt and took the dragon's limp head into her hands, shock chilling her skin. It was Ruda's younger brother, Zori.

Stones and Blackwater, he looked more like her every day.

Ruda, an older youngling and proud sister, had often helped Helena the healer upstairs in the apothecary chamber. She held a special place in Vahly's heart, as they'd spent time picking lavender for Helena in the meadows. Ruda was the one who'd spoken up when others didn't ask the tough questions. And Ruda did a fantastic job with medicines and with rounding up the other younglings when it was needed. Ruda loved Zori dearly. He was incredibly shy, Ruda's opposite, and he rarely left their family's chambers. Ruda had talked endlessly about Zori's knack with jewelry.

Zori's pulse beat sluggishly, and his normally bright, sky blue scales had gone brittle around the edges. Arc gently lifted one of his eyelids. The youngling pulled away weakly but not before they'd seen his eyes. They'd gone completely red, like red hat flowers but bloodied and leaking.

"No…" Vahly clutched the dragon to her and shut her eyes against it all. This had to be killing Ruda.

Kyril clicked, feet shuffling behind Vahly, the bulk of him still in the corridor. He showed her an image of Ruda working alongside Helena.

Vahly and Nix helped Zori into a more comfortable

position in one of the only spots left in the great hall. Arc removed his cloak and set it under Zori's head. Love suffused Vahly at the tender way Arc made certain the clasp didn't scratch Zori's ailing, fragile scales.

Nix gave Vahly one more quick hug, then hurried off to help with another dragon across the hall.

Arc stood over Zori and locked eyes with Vahly. "We won't be able to heal this. It's..." He glanced at the room of dragons. "It has a deathreach."

"I'm not familiar with the term." But she didn't like how it sounded. At all.

Arc sighed heavily. "Some illnesses, some conditions... they reach right into death. There is no... I don't know the right word to use in dragon. When we use our magic to heal, we separate the living flesh and blood from death's decay. There is no separation in this plague. We can treat symptoms, but only the strongest will survive once they are taken under."

Was that scene from today? she asked Kyril. *Is Ruda with Helena on the upper levels?*

Earth magic hit Vahly's chest like a giant fist. She doubled over, not hurting exactly but stunned at its insistency.

"Vahly?" Arc put a hand on her back and Kyril squawked, startling the dragons.

Vahly's magic was demanding that she run from here with Kyril and get to the Lost Valley. Now.

There were dead and dying Lapis everywhere. She couldn't leave them. Not until they had this plague under control. She just couldn't.

Taking a deep breath, she imagined her magic easing

into a calm rhythm. "I'm pretty sure I'm being torn in half," she said, only partly joking. "My power wants me at the Lost Valley, at my birthplace. Kyril too. But I can't just go…"

Staring out over the bodies, she swallowed, her throat tight.

Arc nodded, his face grave. "It's your decision."

But it was no decision at all. Her heart was here, in the Lapis palace with her dragons.

The next hours were filled not with a happy reunion with the Lapis, but with crushing moments that left Vahly gasping with new pain. They found Linexa, the younglings' nursemaid, dead in a corridor on the seventh level. Ruda appeared in Helena's apothecary, and they had to inform her that Zori had the plague and was currently resting in the great hall. Since the sea kynd had once had a similar sickness, Vahly questioned Ryton about a cure. But there was none.

"We lost folk by the hundreds." Ryton leaned against the bars of his cage as the moon rose into the cloudy sky above Red Meadow and threw Vahly's shadow over his small prison. "And the ones who survived were often infertile."

Vahly left him, no words in her to ask anything else. She'd worked her hands to bleeding feeding the sick, moving the dead to the burning place on the upper level beyond Amona's chambers, and twisting the pestle in the mortar to make more poultices and salves.

At last, Vahly found Amona outside the apothecary. Her

mother's eyes were drawn and her face wan. Thankfully, Amona was not sick, but she certainly looked tired to the bone.

They didn't speak. They only held on to one another under the Lapis symbol carved into the lintel.

The night bled on, a blur of meeting old friends and watching them hurry here and there to help their loved ones. Vahly felt raw, turned inside out.

She collapsed in a heap beside Zori and Ruda. She needed to leave now. Astraea would come for her. And for the Lapis. Vahly had to take Kyril and get to the Lost Valley and find her birthplace. Her earth magic shoved against her breastbone and tugged that particular spot below her heart.

But she couldn't keep her eyes open any longer.

Sleep dragged her into a dreamless void.

CHAPTER TWENTY-FIVE

In a wash chamber near the Lapis palace's great hall, Nix poured fresh water into the basin and picked up the soap Helena had made to fight the strange plague. They still didn't know what the illness was or what caused it. More were sickened every day. More deaths. More grieving. Between helping here and managing the needs of her Call Breakers, Nix was bone tired. She hadn't even had time to find another to follow Miren and see what she was getting into. Aitor had been on the trail, but he'd fallen ill after eating here and—

Nix dropped the soap into the basin.

None of her Call Breakers were sick except those who'd eaten here.

Dashing out of the wash chamber, Nix barreled into a male Lapis carrying a tray of sliced apples.

Nix gripped the male's shirt. "Where is your kitchen?"

"Wh-what?"

"Kitchen. Where?"

"That way. There." He pointed, and Nix flew down the corridor, leaving him openmouthed.

The sound of clanging dishes and a commanding male voice drew Nix around a tight corner where the wall opened into a kitchen the size of the entire cider house. A stone table ran the length of the room, copper pots hung from black hooks on the walls, and knives in every shape and size sat in tidy lines near a massive set of crockery. There was a back door leading outside. It wasn't huge, but it was large enough for a full-sized dragon to enter with a hefty load.

"Take them now!" a male Lapis pointed a thick finger at a row of servants, his eyes opened wide. "Well? What are you waiting on? An engraved invitation?" His forehead creased into an array of deep wrinkles, and he swore at the lot, not even noticing Nix.

Nix held up her hands. "Chef, I must speak with you before anyone else leaves this kitchen."

His nostrils flared as she walked around the servants. "And who are you?"

"That's Mistress Nix of the cider house," a mousy servant whispered. "The mistress of the Call Breakers."

The chef rolled his eyes. "Get out of my kitchen. I have no time for your nonsense. We have dragons to tempt into eating so they don't starve!"

"I think the food is exactly what is killing them."

"What are you talking about?" The male's tone was sharp, but fear shadowed his features.

"Can we speak privately?"

His face slammed shut like a door in a windstorm. "No.

I have a job to do. I know what your type is like. Always causing chaos. Go," he ordered the servants.

She wouldn't be able to stop them without attacking the chef, so she let them go. She wasn't sure her hunch was correct. Right now, she had no evidence, not even a shred of it. The only thing dragging her in here was a cold worry chilling her insides.

Hurrying to the chef's side, she hissed at him. "You had best listen to me, fool. None of my Call Breakers have the plague, none except those who ate here."

The chef cocked his head. He pulled a large, skin-bound book from under the stone table. He put a meaty hand on the book's cover. "This is my record of deliveries and staff."

Nix bumped him aside with a hip and threw the book open.

"Now, see here—"

"Your matriarch and I are pretty close these days, chef. I think she'd chuck you if I said you'd poisoned the clan."

The chef swallowed loudly and stepped back.

Nix flipped past a cover page with the Lapis symbol and found the book was arranged from back to front with the most recent items noted in the first quarter of the tome. She ran a talon down today's page but saw nothing out of the ordinary. *Venison from Lapis hunters. Vegetables brought in by Lapis. Apples…*

Nix's talon cut into the page.

Apples brought in by a Call Breaker.

She locked eyes with the chef. "Who brought the apples? I didn't approve of any shipments." Baww might have done so in her absence, but it was unlikely, as they usually brought a full load at mid-season and end of season. They didn't bother with a mere basket. It would feed but a few.

"I...one of yours."

Nix exhaled in a gust. "Yes. I see that. But were you here? Who brought them?"

"She has been coming often. We thought it had been approved. She had your seal on her agreement."

Throat dry, Nix tried to imagine who it could be and why. And if it was possible that whoever was bringing the unapproved fruits was the one poisoning the Lapis. None of this made sense.

But only one dragon stood out in Nix's mind.

The light from the back door went dark as a figure walked quickly inside.

Nix looked up to see Miren standing there with a basket of Call Breaker apples, their specific shade of red like fresh blood.

Nix slid the chef's book toward him. Miren stared, a rabbit caught in the lion's gaze. "I will take care of this, chef. Find all the apples in the castle and make sure they are destroyed and buried. See that you serve no more. I will meet you in Matriarch Amona's chambers in one hour."

The chef ran from the kitchen.

Nix walked slowly toward Miren, not looking forward to what would have to follow this revelation.

Miren dropped the apples and launched out of the back door, taking off into the sky.

Nix followed, flying fast and catching up to her with little effort. Nix grabbed Miren's wing and dragged her to the ground, tossing her to the dirt of the path that led to the sea cliffs.

"I don't care what you do to me," Miren spat. She scrambled to her feet, eyes bright with fury.

"I care about you, Miren. Did you poison the Lapis?" But how could she act against Vahly's clan after taking the blood oath in the Red Meadow alongside everyone else?

"They took my sister from me!" Her wings spread wide, and sparks crackled between her pink lips. "They stole our bond and threw her into war too early, and now she is dead. It is their fault!" Miren marched toward Nix, then stared into her face, nose brushing Nix's. "She wanted to break the Call. She was going to join us. But they found out, and they sent her to the front. Maur and Amona, they sent her on a suicide mission!"

Nix didn't flinch as Miren's sparks flickered over her cheeks and chin. "So why didn't you stop at Maur? Was that not revenge enough?"

"I wanted Amona to suffer." The fire in Miren seemed to die, and she dropped back a step, her gaze going to the ground. "I wanted to watch them die. To hear them groan in pain like my sister. I want them to hurt. All of them."

"Well, you certainly accomplished that goal."

Miren's eyes flashed. "What are you going to do about it? Are you so loyal to the Lapis now that you'll turn one of your own over to them?" She almost seemed triumphant.

But that wasn't at all what Nix had in mind. "No, darling. That is not what's going to happen here."

"Then what? You're going to let me go?"

"Did you not make an oath to the Earth Queen? I would suppose that murdering her clan members would break such a promise, and the breaking would burn through your heart."

Miren began to say something, but Nix cut her off.

"No, I know. You made no such oath. You acted at making the promise that day in the Red Meadow. You lied in body and soul. And now you've killed hundreds of your own kynd, Miren. Hundreds. And younglings too. They had no part in what happened to your sister. No, I will not turn you over. You will receive your punishment as a true clanless one from another clanless one. Get on your knees."

Miren stumbled back. "Wait. Nix. Euskal will never forgive you."

"I must suffer that grief. You have done that too. This is your fault, dear, not mine. I am only cleaning up this mess. I will make it fast. Take your punishment and be glad of it, for Amona would do far worse before she saw you dead at her feet."

Miren was crying, kneeling. A part of Nix raged against this, but duty called, and she had promised to answer.

"You, Miren, are a traitor to your own kynd, to the clanless, and to your Earth Queen. You have caused Vahly, Earth Queen and my dearest friend, grief. For that there must be a reckoning."

Nix drew her dagger and drove it into Miren's eye.

The traitor fell, and Nix walked away, having no desire to see that dagger ever again.

CHAPTER TWENTY-SIX

Vahly's magic grew more and more unwieldy, urging her to hurry to the Lost Valley, to feel the presence of the place where she'd first drawn breath, to…to do what? She didn't know.

At dawn, she joined Arc, took up a bow, and headed out to hunt for food to feed the sick dragons.

The moment the sea's breeze hit her nose, the earth magic's drumming increased tenfold. Gritting her teeth against the tug in her middle, she listened to Arc tell the tale of the first Elven King. She knew he was trying to keep her distracted, and she appreciated it.

"And the legends claim he swam in the ocean every morning at sunrise, that he befriended every beast under the waves and spoke their tongues. Every tree spoke to him, in their own manner, and by touch he could tell you a plant's ability to destroy or heal."

"Did this shining example of a creature have a name? Betterthanus? Or perhaps Impossiblegoals?"

A dimple appeared in Arc's cheek. The pre-dawn's pale yellow light cloaked the dark shirt he wore today and touched the straight line of his nose. "He is only called The First One."

"Yeah, that seems about right. Who would bother with a name that anyone else might pick up down the way? Stick with a title no one can take."

Arc shook his head, and his chest moved in a quiet laugh that Vahly was pleased to see, even in her current state of trying not to run screaming for the Lost Valley.

They took up a spot behind a stand of tall brazenberry bushes that had gone wild, then they nocked an arrow each. Falling into silence, waiting for the deer to show, Vahly's magic became more difficult to ignore. Her hands shook on the bow, so she gripped it harder, willing herself to remain in control.

There, Arc said in her mind.

A stag with wide antlers strolled out of the trees beside the Silver River and into the meadow like he owned the place. The animal was quartered away from them, exposing its side at an angle. Arc raised his bow and Vahly did too, both aiming for the deer as two does trotted into view. One doe faced them head-on while the other gave a clear, broad side opening.

Arc's stillness could've beat a stone's effort at the task. He wasn't even breathing. Only his magic moved, swirling like a storm around his head, almost invisible as he drew the string toward his pointed ear, his muscles bunching beneath his rolled-up sleeves.

Which one? he asked telepathically.

Go for the stag. You're a better shot. I'll get the doe.

Arc whispered three words in elvish and let the arrow fly.

Vahly's arrow hit the doe just below the midline and it fell, mouth gaping open then clamping shut. Arc's stag was dead before it fell.

After dressing the deer, they headed back toward the palace with a pallet of joints for the ailing dragons who were unable to hunt for themselves or those who were too busy to hunt because they were caring for others.

At the steps of the palace, the earth magic stopped Vahly abruptly. A lightning bolt of power seared its way from her feet to the crown of her head, and she called out, dropping the pallet's branch handle. Her hands were sweating, and she felt like she was going to lose what little she had in her belly.

Arc set their burden down and came around to look her in the face. "Vahly, you have to leave. If your power is urging you like this, you should listen. Don't you agree? The dragons still have healthy ones among them. Your absence won't change the outcome overmuch."

"But Amona and Nix—"

"Need you to continue your journey," Amona said, walking out of the shadow of the mountain, the golden Lapis symbols embroidered on her dress's hem sparkling in the rising sun.

Ryton—still caged beside the stairs—stood slowly, his gaze on Amona. He was too far away for Vahly to see what emotion his eyes showed, but from the way he gripped the iron bars, his elbows high and his shoulders drawn up, it surely wasn't happiness or regret.

Nix walked beside Amona. "Kyril is on his way out.

I'm ready to go." She was indeed wearing her travel clothes again, including the trousers she disliked so much. "I'm sure Arc can be ready as soon as he has a word with Rigel."

Arc crouched and dug up a dormant red hat flower—roots and dirt and all. He placed it in Vahly's hand. Earth magic surged from the cool dirt and the spindly roots, and Vahly welcomed the energy into herself, taking comfort from the feel of its power and familiarity.

"What do you think is the right move, Queen Vahly?" The wind teased his ebony hair. "This is your choice. Your move."

Vahly felt like she was being ripped at the seams, torn in all directions. "Astraea could attack at any moment. I need to follow my magic."

A small voice pealed from the palace doors. Ruda scrambled down the stairs, and Kyril flew out of the archway behind her, making Ruda appear as tiny as a rabbit. Kyril flashed Vahly an image of Ruda's brother, Zori, looking much better.

Kyril landed beside Vahly in a gust of wing-swept air, and Ruda hurried up.

"Before you go, will you please consider my plea?" Ruda clasped her hands together, looking nervous.

"Is Zori feeling any better?"

Ruda smiled widely. "He is."

A weight lifted off Vahly's shoulders. "I'm so glad. Now what's this about a plea?"

"Can I be Kyril's Sourceparent?"

The young dragon wanted to be the one to care for Kyril in the case of Vahly's death, the stand-in for Kyril's parents.

The request touched Vahly's heart, and she smiled, watching Ruda's loving gaze flick to Kyril.

Vahly put a hand on Ruda's small shoulder. The dragon's scales were cool to the touch. Thankfully, Ruda hadn't caught the plague. Vahly looked up and met Nix's eyes. Nix felt like Vahly's Sourceparent, though they'd never gone through the ceremony. Nix's lips tucked into a line, and she cocked her midnight blue head. Vahly sighed, fate heavy on her shoulders.

"Ruda, I would love to make you Kyril's Sourceparent."

Ruda beamed, dimples tucking into her sky blue cheeks and happiness sparking in her slitted, yellow eyes.

A strange wind rose, and the smell of the ocean drove out the scent of earth. Vahly tensed, gaze snapping to Amona.

Vahly knew well they had no time for this, but she couldn't stand to break Ruda's heart, not with all the youngling had been going through. No, Vahly wouldn't refuse this request. The ceremony would happen, and all the world could wait on it.

CHAPTER TWENTY-SEVEN

After handing the deer they'd slain over to the Lapis butchers, Vahly, Arc, Nix, Kyril, and Ruda gathered in the Red Meadow, leaving Ryton in his iron cage. Vahly still had no idea why her earth magic wished for her to keep the sea kynd alive and nearby.

She and the others made a circle near the Silver River, not far from where the Spirit of the River had appeared before they'd headed into the western mountains to find Kyril.

What surprises did the Lost Valley have in store for them? And how were they going to get there when it was covered in salt water and churning with vicious sea creatures?

Vahly pushed the worries away and placed a hand on Kyril.

Are you good with this, Kyril? she asked.

He showed her an image of Ruda bringing him a bowl of water that was over half her size, muscles straining and face tight with the effort. What a kind little thing Ruda was.

Then Vahly saw an image of Ruda combing out Kyril's pelt and Kyril carrying Zori closer to the earthblood vents in the great hall.

She guessed all of that meant yes, he certainly was.

Vahly set her other hand on Ruda's forehead. "I mark Ruda of Clan Lapis as Sourceparent for my familiar, Kyril of the West. If I should die, she will rear him until adulthood and will support him. In turn, he will treat her with the respect owed a proper parent or familiar, seeing to her needs above all others save my own as long as we live."

Magic shivered up Vahly's feet and hummed through her body, zinging down her arms and into Ruda, who gasped, eyes going wide, and Kyril, who shuffled his feathers. Vahly could feel the bond that buzzed between Ruda and Kyril, though it had no tug on her.

Arc placed a fisted hand over his heart and bowed to them both while Nix blasted triumphant dragonfire into the air above the group.

Vahly ran a hand along the storm-blue feathers near Kyril's sunny beak. "Congratulations. You have a Sourceparent, my lovely. And well you deserve such a one as Ruda." Vahly glanced over her shoulder to see Ruda absolutely beaming.

"And now," Vahly said, taking the weight of what was to come onto her shoulders, "we head under the waves once again to fight." Her magic pushed against her chest, bringing the scent of the sea to her nose and the image of Ryton into her mind. "First, I must get the key to Ryton's cage."

Ruda gave Kyril one last embrace, then took off into the

sky, hurrying back to the palace ahead of them, her wings a match to the sky's pale light.

Nix straightened her traveling cloak and adjusted her Lapis ring, apparently enjoying the way it reflected the light. "I really don't see how the sea kynd can help."

"I don't either, but my magic says he must stay nearby. It might not be a "help" sort of situation. Maybe he'll serve as bait."

Arc's eyebrow lifted. "Truly?"

"For the Sea Queen," Vahly said. "He is her consort as well as her general, and he betrayed her. She'll want to eat him alive."

Nix laughed. "Now I'm in." She rubbed her hands, her talons clicking together. "May I tell him the news? Pretty please, Queenie?"

Vahly shook her head. "You're incorrigible."

Arc nudged Vahly with an elbow. "And you're not?"

"Oh, I'm completely incorrigible, but I haven't had an extra fifty or so years to grow up." Vahly bit her lip, hiding a laugh.

Nix's mouth popped open and she stopped, hands on her hips. "You have no idea how old I am, girl."

"I have a good guess."

Nix narrowed her eyes, giving Vahly a chill even though she was her dearest friend. "And what happens to those who leak information about me?"

Vahly chuckled. "They soon also leak blood."

Nix strolled past them, then took off into the sky. "Don't forget that, Queen Vahly. If anyone can get around an oath to teach someone a much-needed lesson, it's me."

Arc tsked at her as she flew toward the Lapis palace.

"Let's hurry," Vahly said, waving Kyril over.

Kyril bent to let Vahly climb up, and Vahly held a hand to Arc.

"You're certain?" Arc's gaze traveled from Vahly to Kyril's face.

Kyril dipped his head lower.

"I think he is willing." Vahly gripped Arc's warm, strong hand, and Arc launched into place behind her.

Kyril ran a few steps, then rose into the air, his wings beating silently. The ground dropped away, and Vahly held tightly to the furry ruff at his neck.

Arc leaned into Vahly's back. She thrilled at the feel of his powerful legs pressing against hers and the sensation of his warmth easing into her body. Twisting, she glanced at him. He wore a sad grin, his crown flickering at the edges of her vision. His presence overwhelmed her, and she simply wanted to stare.

"I want to gawk at your handsome self, but it's killing my neck." She grinned at him and turned back around.

Suddenly, the air behind her went cold and Arc was in front of her, facing her, his legs beneath hers and his hands on her sides.

"What? How?"

He chuckled. "You look so shocked. Is it such a surprise that the Elven King can move more quickly than your human eyes can see?"

Vahly swallowed and kept her fingers in Kyril's fur. Arc was just ridiculously beautiful in addition to being one of the very few people who knew all her challenges and shortcomings and loved her anyway.

Kyril veered away from the palace, doing a slow loop.

Arc grinned. "Why do you think he's giving us some time?"

Vahly leaned forward and lifted her chin so that her mouth was close to Arc's. Her body broke out in goosebumps as his hands moved to her hips. In the middle of all this grief, all this terror of what was to come, this was life. Vahly wasn't about to let the moment go.

She let go of Kyril and put her hands on either side of Arc's face. His jawbone was sharp under her palms. As she drew his mouth to hers, his eyes fluttered closed. Pleasure bursting through her body, she moved her lips over his, savoring the heat and the magic that was all his. His arms went around her body, almost too tightly, and he pulled her fully onto his lap as Kyril spread his wings, soaring evenly. Vahly, still cradling Arc's head, felt the tips of his pointed ears, and air magic roared around them, the sound overcoming all. Arc kissed her deeply. She felt his love for her suffuse the movements of his fingers on her ribs and the caress of his mouth.

Stones and Blackwater, how she loved him.

Kyril dipped toward the palace and they broke apart, gasping and smiling.

Arc wiggled his eyebrows, then leapt from Kyril's back, landing far below on the palace steps, not even faltering for a moment in a jump that would've killed most. He looked up at her as Kyril landed. The sun poured over Arc's crowned head and brilliant face, lighting him up like fire burned inside him, bright and strong.

As soon as she'd dismounted, Vahly felt the urge to bow to Arc. "You need to stop Elven King-ing so much," she said, slapping his arm as she walked past. "I want to go to my knees for you when you look like that, and bowing isn't really my style."

Arc's head fell back as he laughed, then he bowed to her. "Apologies, my queen. I must confess the idea of it has its temptations."

Vahly snorted and reached back to pinch his thigh, wishing they could go on joking and flirting.

Instead, she had to find a key to free her enemy and dive back into the reach of the Sea Queen's foul magic.

CHAPTER TWENTY-EIGHT

Astraea sped through the water with two hundred warriors and General Venu at her back. She'd called the Watcher to her chambers after the carving of Grystark and Ryton appeared at her door, and the Seer's words gnawed at Astraea's mind.

"The one with the shadowed heart gathers allies. I see the darkness falling in on her love. Another listened, understood. He too is gone," the Watcher had said that night, the scars across the place where her eyes had once been twitching as she bent over her scrying bowl.

Darkness falling. That had sounded exactly like a rock fall, like the disaster inside the tunnel where Grystark had died. The shadowed heart had to be his wife, Lilia, and the one who'd listened to Lilia's complaints had to be Ryton.

Lilia had left that carving for Astraea.

What kind of allies could she possibly gather? None of the sea folk would rise against their queen, especially for a weakened and scarred one such as Lilia.

The water went cold as they dove past a blood-red

forest of coral with branches as thin and twisted as the Watcher's arms. Venu caught up to Astraea; his nostrils and gills flared and his eyes flashed with righteous anger. The general said little, but he was obviously appalled at the outcome of events. He was one of the very few Astraea had seen fit to fully inform.

"The one with the shadowed heart plots near the cursed place," the Watcher had said.

Astraea knew of two places where Lilia might be hiding out, and they were on their way to the second possibility. The first guess had eaten up three days of searching, two days Astraea should have been going after Ryton and that Earth Queen. But if there were rebels here under the sea, they had to be annihilated first. There could be no discord in the ranks when they attacked the land again.

Following the cold, northern current, they swam toward a tower of blackened rock. The tower had once spouted Blackwater, giving power to the first of the sea kynd. The well had gone dormant, and an eerie silence reigned now, filled with phantoms of those lost during the dark time between this Blackwater dying away and the next being discovered near Tidehame. Sea folk did not come here.

Unless they were planning dark deeds.

At the mouth of a great sea cave, Astraea held up a hand to instruct one half of the force to circle around to a back entrance that scouts had detailed in their report.

Astraea swam to the seabed and walked beside General Venu to the mouth of the cave, where voices trickled from the darkness.

Lifting her spear, Astraea strode into the cave to see a crowd of her own folk clustered around Lilia. The sparkling glow of gold and black seaweed waved across their upturned faces, and the sight choked Astraea.

"What a tragedy," she said.

Those gathered gasped, and Lilia whirled, the scars from her punishment moon-white on her face and her hair floating around her head like rays of a dark sun. Such a shame for a beauty like her to be ruined. But that's what happened when one wed a traitor.

Astraea studied every face, memorizing who was here. Rage sizzled in her veins and behind her eyes. Her knuckles cracked as she gripped her spear.

"We have a war on our hands," she hissed. "Our end churns like a whirlpool at our feet, the Earth Queen has risen, and here you are, plotting against your savior."

Lilia straightened and raised her chin. "You are not our savior. You killed innocent sea folk with your mad plans. You don't care about us! You only care for your pride and power."

Fury tumbling through her vision like a red cloud, Astraea spoke a spell over her spear's shimmering tip, and a current rocked the cave, driving the rebels into the walls. Heads cracked and blood flowed as a full fight erupted.

Venu's unit swam like eels, quick and clever, under the crowd, surprising them with spells and physical strikes.

Some of the rebels fled through the back of the cave where the second half of Astraea's force waited. Shrieks tore the sea.

Had Lilia gone down?

Astraea looked left and right, unable to tell in the bloodied water and the chaos. She slipped out the front, pushed past two males locked in combat, and swam over the cave toward the back, only to see a flash of movement in the distance.

Lilia had fled along with a small group of followers.

Astraea began to cast a spell, to drive them high, then smash them against the land, but she held herself back. She wanted to send assassins for them. To be rid of them quietly. None had to know they lived still and that there was any sort of rebellion afoot.

To think Lilia believed she could thwart Astraea. It was laughable. So entertaining, in fact, that Astraea smiled the entire swim back to the castle.

Soon, the entire world would see Astraea's full power.

Actually, today seemed as good a day as any to get started.

"Venu," she called as the general joined her and the warriors escorting her home. "Today, we will set out for the Lapis territory. Tomorrow, we attack. Make ready."

"Yes, of course. As you wish, my queen." Venu veered right and went to work, calling out orders for those who could best multiply the salt water and command the tides.

"It would've been better with you here, Ryton," Astraea whispered to herself. "It's sad indeed that once I find you, I will have to kill you. Such a waste."

CHAPTER TWENTY-NINE

Ryton held on to one of the crystal spikes on the back of the dragon—Nix, they called her—as the group flew toward the Lost Valley. Every inch of his skin crawled. How could he ride a dragon after all they'd taken from his kynd?

Something the land kynd called sweat rolled off his body as he gritted his teeth, wishing his coral spear was strapped to his back instead of to the elf's. The Elven King rode behind Vahly on the enormous gryphon, a creature from Ryton's childhood nightmares. That thing could take his head off with one easy bite.

But the worst that Ryton had experienced since coming onto land was the moment he'd finally seen Matriarch Amona, the evil dragon queen who'd killed Selene.

His fingers shook and his knuckles went white.

He'd thought his rage had fallen away with his hope to return to the sea, but it lived, bright and fierce inside his veins, stirred back to life by Amona's calm demeanor and the way she acted like a mother to the Earth Queen. How could anyone take comfort from that beast?

He wanted her dead.

The sound of waves crashed in his ears, and a tingling spread from his heart to his limbs. Swallowing, he loosened his grip on the dragon's spike.

His magic did not want Amona dead.

But how could that be? She was the enemy of the ocean, and water magic was born of the sea. It made no sense.

It was one thing for both his magic and the memory of his curious, merciful sister to stay his hand when it came to the young Earth Queen, one who wished to balance the world. Perhaps she would be good and show kindness and only seek to defeat Astraea instead of wiping the salt water from the world completely as he'd feared for so long.

But Amona? There was no reason for his water magic to restrain him with regard to her safety. She had to die for what she'd done.

Magic rushed up his neck, gagging him.

No. It couldn't be. But there was no denying it. The power of the ocean wanted him to aid Vahly, not to focus on finding a way to murder Amona.

He shut his eyes, feeling the raw air peeling away his sea kynd ways. Tears threatened, but he fought them and won, opening his eyes only when the dragon began her descent.

They alighted gently, about twenty feet from the lapping waves of the Lost Valley, the last place human kynd had lived.

The dragon shifted form, then began to dress, mumbling to herself. "Sea germs all over me. When did I sign up for this job?" Then her bright eyes narrowed at Ryton. "You were certainly tense up there, General. Better stay in line with our plans, or you'll find out how quickly I can burn you alive in my human form. The Elven King is fond of experiments, and I think he'd appreciate that one."

"I'm not killing anyone. My magic won't allow it." The dragon language tasted foul on his tongue.

Vahly approached, the gryphon in her wake. "What was that about your magic?"

Her face was impassive, unreadable. He wished she weren't so good at hiding her feelings.

"I was telling Nix that my magic urges me to aid you." They didn't need to know everything. If he could find a way to kill Amona without injuring himself or damaging his magic, he would. He wouldn't give up on it yet. But even as he thought about the killing, his chest tightened uncomfortably.

"Is the beast bothering you?" Vahly jabbed her chin in the direction of the black creature on Ryton's back.

"Always," he said, allowing her mistaken guess to hide his truth. It wasn't as if the creature didn't bother him. It did, every single second of every single day. He felt like his skin had been peeled away and his heart beat on the outside of his body, like he should have been dead long ago and this creature had kept him from death for some sick feeding of its desire.

"I honestly don't know how to use you in this quest, General Ryton." Vahly scratched her head as Arcturus headed toward them, away from where he'd been studying the water.

"The currents flow east, then south," the Elven King

said. His face was full of power and a frightening calm that reminded Ryton of Amona. Did these land kynd not show their emotions? They were such cold beings. "I can work my magic on you again," the elf said to Vahly.

Nix nudged Arcturus's head with a wingtip. "I bet you could." She winked.

The corner of Vahly's mouth lifted, but she paced, her mind obviously elsewhere. "I have to take Kyril, but I don't know that he can swim."

"I'd say he'd be able to," Arcturus replied. "Though he'll probably hate it."

Vahly shrugged and petted the gryphon's leg. "We'll give it a try, all right?"

Kyril squawked, and they walked toward the edge of the water.

"I'll fly high and keep an eye out," Nix said. She flew into the sky, and Ryton wondered if she knew his kynd would see her from a good mile off if they were looking.

The Elven King stood closer to Ryton, removing the coral spear and whispering an elvish spell over it. "And I'll remain here with Ryton in case he comes up with a way to help."

Anger burned its way across Ryton's chest. "Please do not bespell my personal weapon, elf."

"Desperate times, General. Forgive the disrespect, but I must ensure my queen's safety as best as I am able."

"She is not your queen." Ryton felt powerless, like he was swimming right into the main western current with no hope of breaking through the ocean's tug toward the empty sea. He wanted to strike back somehow, to hurt someone, to feel something else. So he hit low, right where it would injure this proud land kynd. "You have no queen."

Arcturus's lips parted and a breath left him like Ryton had thrust his spear through his gut. Then the elf straightened and locked gazes with Ryton. A deep and aged power swirled in the depths of the Elven King's eyes.

"You will never speak of my kin again," the elf whispered, following the phrase with a loud elvish spell. The king's hands moved, the brightness of noonday and the black of night tracing their shape.

Air magic blew across Ryton's flesh. Ryton froze, and the sound of wind rushing above water deafened him. Heat sparked across his mouth and traveled down his throat. He gripped his neck, desperate to breathe, wishing his gills would work here, longing for the water.

Finally, the spell relented. Ryton sagged, going to his knees. "What did you do to me?"

"As I said, you will not speak of them again. Ever. You are unable."

Ryton wouldn't give him the satisfaction of trying.

Vahly's voice called from the shoreline. "What are you two doing?"

"Come," Arcturus ordered Ryton.

Ryton had little choice but to obey even though every bit of him fought the situation, his mind splashing through idea after idea. He was at war with himself. Wanting to help the Earth Queen but also wanting to spare Lilia and Echo and the other good ones of his kynd.

The Elven King worked his air magic, mixed with some blood sorcery. With his long fingers, he painted Vahly and her gryphon familiar with sparking light, squid-ink darkness, and his bitter-scented royal blood.

Vahly and the gryphon were set to travel into the flooded valley.

"Perhaps I am meant to go with her?" Ryton asked, his voice weak from whatever Arcturus had done to him.

Vahly faced him, blood staining her eyelids, forehead, and cheeks. "Not yet. I don't trust you in your own element. If I get desperate, I'll let you know."

Ryton's heart cinched at the blend of ferocity and innocence in her eyes, so much like Selene's. How did one manage innocence when one had been to war and killed? It was another kind of magic, a perpetual cleansing of the soul, some nightly ritual only a few had the power to enact. "If you see long fish with yellow and black markings, hold very still. They will pass if they don't see you move."

Vahly blinked and rubbed a bit of dirt from her chin. "And if they do?"

"They swarm and you both die. Their teeth hold a venom that not even I can withstand."

With a curt nod, Vahly turned away. Then she and the gryphon dove, and Ryton remained on the land, drying out like a fish left for the birds.

CHAPTER THIRTY

Every muscle in Vahly's body bunched as she dove into the water. Kyril, cutting the water with his beak and his wings tucked tightly at his sides, flashed images of them flying.

Yes, that would be far nicer. But we must focus on our job here, love. I know this fully reeks of the worst nightmares, but we must soldier on. Now, watch for other beasts like the ones Ryton mentioned.

A fine grit clouded the water, and Vahly could only see a few feet in front of them as they swam toward the center of the civilization. A cluster of buildings made of stacked stone circled a cleared area where three large boulders stood. The structures were missing some walls and all of their roofs. The boulders brought the Source's Blackwater spring to mind.

Imagined memories surfaced inside Vahly's mind, the daydreams she'd crafted for herself as a child. Her mother cradling her and singing a lilting tune, the skin on her arms like Vahly's, unscaled and soft to the touch. A game between older children that involved kicking a ball of rags down a road, plenty of playful shoving required. And the crackling of a fire in a small hearth, one sized for humans, not dragons.

Vahly's magicked breath hitched, and she swallowed her sadness like a tonic. It would help her feel her way to her home.

Magic tugged on the invisible link below Vahly's heart, urging her to go quickly. Was the magic simply impatient to see Vahly endowed with more power, or was there another immediate reason for haste? Did the magic know something that Vahly did not?

Pushing panic away with thoughts of Arc on shore, ready to give help, and Nix soaring above, watching out for them, Vahly swam on.

Beside her, Kyril swam, eyes narrowed and furred paws dashing through the foggy salt water in an almost desperate fashion. His tail flicked behind him, drawing the occasional small and curious fish.

They passed another circle of stacked stone houses as well as a rockfall, originating from a sea shelf that had collapsed during the flooding. The pile of bruise-dark rock reached from this second collection of structures to another that was difficult to see in the murky water. Shapes flitted in and out of the rockfall, their bodies catching the light.

Vahly gripped Kyril's pelt. *Stay clear of the fall there. See the fish?*

The shapes swimming around the spot were just as Ryton had described, sleek and striped like hornets.

They swam on, her magic pulling her in what felt like two different directions. She took up the path to the northeast, heading for a larger building surrounded by deep holes. What was the point of the holes? She swam over one, its depths black and still, before heading into the large structure. Clutching the one wall that remained undamaged, she twisted to watch Kyril thrust through the water, catching up. He must've been curious about those fish and had fallen behind. She'd have to keep a closer watch on him. Though he was as big as the largest dragon, he was still young and unexperienced. With Arc's blood painted across his eyes and beak, he looked the part of a warrior. Vahly smiled grimly. And warrior he would be. Pride lifted a fraction of the weight off her shoulders.

Kyril treaded water outside the doorway, or what was left of the doorway, as Vahly swam deeper into the large building. Smooth rectangles of a reddish stone marked three places inside the walls. Vahly wiped leafy growth off the first of them and bent, squinting as she tried to read. Sunlight streamed through the water, lighting the etched words with undulating threads of gold.

Vahly couldn't fluently speak her own kynd's language, but she could read most of it. The tongue wasn't too different from dragon. The first inscription was a name. Basajaun. The name meant Old Man of the Woods and was tied to a folktale, the details of which Vahly couldn't recall. Tally marks showed a large number. Ah. It was the year and season. A long while back. And there was another word. What did *hil* mean? A chill slithered down her back.

Death.

This was a record of the dates this Basajaun had lived. So was this large structure a burial place? That didn't seem right. Humans buried their dead, did they not? Perhaps he was buried under this place? Vahly knelt and placed a hand against the packed ground, bubbles gathering around her fingers. She tried to feel the death in the earth beneath her palm, but the magic was dulled by the water.

Kyril, I need you.

Kyril ducked his head into the structure, the three remaining walls too tight for his entire body. Vahly touched his head and felt their bond zip through her arm and into her heart where her magic rose up, awakened by Kyril's presence.

The earth here was blessed; it sang through Vahly's bones, a song she could hear perfectly inside her head. The drumming of earth magic echoed the tune, matching it, strengthening it.

Vahly looked at Kyril. *This is a place of birth, not death.* She touched the marker on the wall again, her toes brushing the sandy ground as she swam closer. *They marked their birthplaces. I must find mine.*

She began to clean off the other markers in the structure, but Kyril nudged her, and her magic pounded through her blood. The pull to leave was unmistakable.

Why did you nudge me? she asked as they swam away from the building. *Can you feel the earth too? Can you feel a tug, an urging in your chest?*

Kyril jerked his head, kicking his feet to swim faster. He sent images of the rising sea into Vahly's mind. The water level at the Lapis coastline was higher than it had been reported just last night.

How do you have that image? she asked.

Then Kyril shared a blink of color that Vahly belatedly realized was Arc's face, seen through the water just after they'd entered the Lost Valley.

Vahly put a hand on Kyril as they swam, hoping the touch would help her communicate with Arc and Nix. *Arc? Can you hear me? Nix?*

I'm here, Queenie, Nix said. *The ocean is lurching like Aitor after he's had too many. You had best hurry up what you're doing down there.*

Do you need me at your side? I can lash Ryton down and dive in. Arc's words sounded stronger than they ever had.

Before Vahly could answer, a current shoved her and Kyril, breaking their contact. Kyril rolled, water foaming around the tips of his wings and claws. His legs churned, his eyes shut as he tried to use his wings to move back to Vahly. But it wasn't working. His wings wouldn't grab the water like they did the air and proved to be a big problem.

Vahly rushed to help him, swam over a cluster of homes, and reached for him. He was nearly to the rockfall where those venomous fish had been earlier. She had his back paw for a moment, fingers curling into his thick fur and her lungs burning with the effort, but then another crash of water gushed through the calmer area and broke them apart.

Kyril thrashed, panicking. He sent her images of them flying, of the two of them talking by the earthblood vent in the great hall beside Zori, and one simply of Vahly's face.

Vahly pushed through the churning water and at last grabbed hold of his pelt fully. The current eased, and they were able to swim normally.

Metallic yellow winked from the rockfall directly below their kicking feet.

And then more yellow. More.

The venomous fish gathered, hundreds of them, their beady eyes trained on Kyril and Vahly. Their black and yellow stripes shot fear through Vahly's chest.

Hold still, Kyril. Just breathe slowly. Very slowly.

The first fish she'd seen twitched its small, flat tail and swam closer. Vahly's heart was coming out of her throat. The fish bumped her bare ankle and she had to fight herself not to move her head and peer down to see if its teeth were about to end this effort far sooner than planned.

What a way to go. Death by wee fishie. Not exactly the queenly sort of exit she'd thought she'd have.

Vahly and Kyril floated, kept from rising to the surface by Arc's air magic blood spell. Vahly's heart knocked one side of her chest and then the other. Kyril wasn't blinking and his chest was still. He wasn't even breathing. The tips of his great wings shivered slightly, his fear apparent. Vahly wanted to attack the fish and scare them off. But Ryton's warning about the venomous fish rang through her head, and he'd saved her once...

The other fish joined the one bumping her ankle. They drifted under her body and Kyril's, scales darkening in the shadows.

At last, the striped fish swam away, into the hazy depths, and Vahly sagged with relief.

Kyril shook his head, and his feathers drew bubbling arcs in the water.

Focusing on the tug, tug, tug of the earth magic in her

chest and the drumming of the power in her blood, she swam down to the rockfall. It sat in a depression in the bedrock and extended three times the length of the cider house.

Stomach sinking, Vahly knew.

Her birthplace lay beneath the immense slabs of dark stone.

This isn't going to be easy, she said to Kyril, reaching for him, swimming a few feet above the rock debris.

He swam closer and let her set a hand on him. Then she summoned her power, trying hard to smell the earth beyond the reach of Arc's spell and the salt water. A thrum of strength pulsed from the bedrock.

"Move," she commanded, spreading her fingers wide and directing her palm and intention toward the rockfall.

The tumble of stone trembled. One large slab slipped from its perch and crashed to the sea floor under Vahly and Kyril. Plumes of sand rose into the water, blinding them.

Panicking, Vahly tried to wave the sand away. They had to keep a watch for more dangerous creatures and sea kynd as well.

When the sand cleared, Vahly tried again. Her lungs began to burn.

Kyril kicked his feet, and his beak parted like he might have been having trouble breathing.

Vahly's body shook in time with the ground, but only a few more rocks fell away from the homes that lay underneath. And the magic was dying. She couldn't take a full breath.

This isn't going to cut it. Gripping Kyril's pelt, she swam over him and took hold of his ruff. *Take us to the surface if you can.*

Kyril lurched through the water, wings and legs struggling against another strong current. They broke the surface, gasping, to see Nix landing beside Ryton and Arc. Ryton looked murderous. Nix looked the same way she had the night they'd accidentally dropped ten bags of coin into the Silver River on their way back from a smuggling trade. Arc stood calmly, his kingly power practically oozing from his pores. The breeze kicked up, and Arc's mint and resin scent rode the wind.

"We need another plan!" Vahly shouted over the waves as she rubbed Arc's blood from her eyes, dashing away the last of the spell.

Nix put a hand on her ample hip. "How about dice and cider until the end comes? Go down in a fire of pleasant entertainment and all that. I bet Arcturus has some idea on how to keep your mind off the brevity of our lifespan. Hmm?"

Arc looked at the ground, a grin rucking up one cheek.

Warmth traveled the length of Vahly's body as she remembered their kiss.

"I might be shirking my duties if I let the land be swamped while I'm betting on seven and nine," Vahly said.

"How about if you put your gold on three? I've always thought that was the true lucky number." Nix stepped back from the shoreline as Vahly and Kyril approached.

Arc helped Vahly off Kyril's back, and soon they were on land and dried by air magic.

Feet on firm ground, Vahly had to restrain herself. She

truly wanted to get on her knees and kiss the earth, but she looked to Ryton.

"It's time for you to show me you deserve to live, General Ryton. And let me tell you, I'm not in the best of moods, so you'd better work to impress."

CHAPTER THIRTY-ONE

As the Earth Queen spoke, Ryton inhaled, the beast on his back clicking like it enjoyed every breath Ryton owed to its existence.

"I need a way to lift a bunch of fallen rock from a group of homes," Vahly said. Blood ran from her nose as if she'd been hit. Most likely the result of being in the water under that spell for too long. Her kynd didn't function well in the sea, just as his didn't on the land. "My birthplace sits beneath the mess," she added. "Kyril and I can't even swim properly with that current that sweeps through there every other minute."

"If your elf removes the stink of his spell from my spear," Ryton said, "I can probably shift the water out of that area."

Vahly's eyes narrowed, and she almost seemed to grow a foot in height. "You will show him respect, General Ryton."

"I don't need anything from him, my queen," Arc said, quiet authority and confidence carrying through his voice.

176

Vahly ignored Arc and stepped up to Ryton, her face inches from his. The scent of the land came off her, turned dirt and roots and four-legged beasts. He could almost hear the gryphon screeching in his mind. Ryton tried to stop inhaling the smell, closing his gills in instinct before correcting himself and flaring his nostrils to no avail.

"I am truly thankful for your help in the sea," the Earth Queen said, "but don't get so comfortable that you think I will put up with insolence. Now, on your knees to my king."

Anger flashed through Ryton. He raised a hand, wanting to strike.

Kyril's wings spread wide, and he stood over Ryton, the gryphon's gaze throwing daggers.

Nix stepped closer and a stream of black smoke drifted between her pearl-white teeth. "Go ahead, fishy. See what happens."

But Arc was the most frightening. He had no need to intimidate with proximity or anything like that. Just standing there, his ability to end Ryton's life in a creative and horrifying way was as clear as if the elf had written the spell on parchment and held it up for all to see.

Ryton reined in his pride and took a knee before the Elven King. "Apologies, King Arcturus."

"Much better," Vahly muttered. "Now, up." She yanked Ryton to standing, her strength surprising, considering her size. "You have work to do. Arc, please give the sea kynd his spear."

Arc spoke another spell over Ryton's beloved scarlet spear, then handed it back. The coral fit to Ryton's grip, and he took simple pleasure in holding it again. Vahly flexed her sword hand, and Ryton realized she hadn't retrieved her weapon.

As he walked toward the water, Vahly beside him and the rest a step behind, he tried to remember the spellwork needed to move a collection of water.

"The sword you lost. Was it as important to you as my spear is to me?"

Vahly's gaze flicked to his face, then away as she stared over the water. Her cheeks were dirty with traces of blood and bits of earth, but it suited her, made her look fierce. She truly did resemble Selene. The spark to her eye. The braid. The line of her nose and jaw. He wanted to hate her, but he couldn't.

"It was a gift from my mother," she said. "It had an ivory hilt."

"I had thought you were taken as a babe…"

"From my dragon mother, Matriarch Amona."

Ryton bristled and cut the conversation off. "You will have until sunset to do what you must."

"Just there." She pointed. "About where we surfaced."

Ryton nodded, swallowing the bitterness that came with aiding the daughter of Amona. "If my guess about my current strength is correct, I won't be able to hold the currents away past sunset. And know this, I could be wrong. This might fail entirely. Or I might succeed, but only for a moment, and then the water will return, and I won't have the ability to stop it, I don't think. Not in my current condition."

Nix leaned in. "And what are we to do once the water is gone? Can you move that rock if the sea is no longer a problem?"

"I'm not certain," Vahly said. "I'll have to work quickly, and the sea bed doesn't obey me like the land does."

Arc wove a sphere of light between his hands. "I can help with removing the rock. Once it's done, you go straight to where your power leads you," he said to Vahly, passing the light to her. "I will help General Ryton control the water. And Nix, I will create a circle of protection around you so that the spelled salt water doesn't touch you."

Ryton whirled. "And how will you manage to do that, Elven King?"

Arcturus smiled like a demon. "You will have to wait and see."

How Ryton loathed that elf. Pushing his anger away, Ryton spoke the spell over his spear. It'd been too long since he'd visited the Blackwater well in Tidehame to renew his strength. The spell felt clumsy and ill-spoken on his lips, but the sound of water magic crashed in his ears all the same, and the buzz of power cloaked the bright red weapon.

He lifted it and pointed the tip at the water, a blend of pride for how Selene's good nature had touched him and horror for how he was helping the enemy swamping him and threatening to drag him under.

"Please don't let this end us all," he whispered.

CHAPTER THIRTY-TWO

Vahly was almost certain Ryton wouldn't turn his spear on her. Not completely.

He raised it high, then aimed at the rockfall, his words slippery and oddly punctuated. The sea folk's language wasn't meant to be spoken on land. Waves peeled away from a circle of space where she and Kyril had surfaced. The tips of gray rock began to peer through the rippling, sweeping salt water, and even Nix looked impressed by Ryton's power. What could only be described as a reverse wave curled from the earth, revealing the entire area, the sides of a few homes visible without the sandy haze of the sea surrounding them.

Magic plucked Vahly's heart, and she grabbed for Kyril. He bumped her hand with his beak and clicked his tongue when she set a hand on his side.

Arc finished his spell for Nix's protection from the spelled salt water. "Come!" He looked like a much younger version of himself as he waved and leapt from the former shoreline. He landed, puffs of sand rising around his boots. The land Ryton had cleared of water was dry.

Ryton lowered his spear. Dark circles had formed under his eyes.

Panic stabbed Vahly, seeing the spear lowered and Arc already using his air magic to move rocks below. The water churned like a living wall, surrounding the cluster of buried structures on three sides. The fourth side was dry all the way to the rocky coast.

"You don't need to keep your weapon raised?" she asked Ryton.

"No. I hold the spell within me now. It will last as long as I do or as long as I will it to."

Vahly met Kyril's gaze. "Grab him. We're taking him with us. If he tries anything funny, take one of his legs off."

Ryton glared. "I heard that."

"I wanted you to."

Kyril's beak clamped down on the shirt the Jades had given to Ryton, then Kyril threw the general so that Ryton landed neatly on the gryphon's back.

Nix—her body and wings cloaked in a transparent, golden orb—followed Kyril and Vahly toward Arc.

Nix eyed the magical sphere around her. "I'm glad Arc has that crown and its magic. This will be powerful against the sea kynd," she whispered to Vahly. "Also, I need to tell you something when you finish your work here."

Vahly frowned at the odd tone of Nix's voice. "You can tell me now if you like. I wouldn't mind a distraction."

"No, this is a big conversation. It must wait, Queenie."

Nodding and watching Kyril's tail flick with nervousness, Vahly walked on. All around them, the water hissed like it was angry at being bossed about. A shiver crawled over Vahly.

Arc moved his hands, and the last of the rocks from the sea shelf shifted to sit beyond the broken homes. None of the roofs remained, and most of the structures were nothing but piles of stone.

Holding her breath, fearing this would go nowhere and that she'd somehow made a huge mistake, Vahly walked toward the first building. "We're looking for a birthplace marker set into the walls. It will state my name and might be made of a different color stone than the structure."

Slick patches of algae grew over the right half of an arched entrance to a three-bedroom home. Or what she guessed was a home. The skeletal remains of four wooden chairs sprawled across the sandy floor. Magic drumming inside her veins and tugging at her chest, she bent to study a carving set into the chair's back. Her fingers traced the curve of a tree branch and the tiny scratches that formed an acorn.

Nix crouched beside Vahly. "An oak. The humans should really have branched out with their decor."

"Sometimes they use stag antlers," Vahly said, wondering who had sat in this chair and if it might have been her own mother. She brushed the chair's broken arm, wishing she could somehow know if her mother's hand had rested here.

Arc scanned the walls, looking for birthplace markers. Vahly was hesitant to look, fearing this was a grand mistake, a waste of time, that she'd misread her magic.

Kyril towered over the home, shuffling his wings every now and then to shake off the water spray. Ryton sat very still on Kyril's back, his strange eyes flicking from Vahly to the open sea beyond his magicked walls.

"Earth Queen, may I join you?" Ryton asked, eyeing Kyril like he might bite his leg off. He wasn't wrong to be concerned.

"Yes," Vahly said.

Ryton slid from Kyril's back.

Arc and Nix flanked Vahly.

"Why do you wish to come?" Vahly asked.

Ryton entered the home. He knelt and gently lifted the sea-eaten back of another chair. "I've always been fascinated with human things. Probably because it is taboo." He pushed a spot on the top of the chair back, and a square of wood swung open.

Vahly rushed over. "What is that?"

Nix and Arc leaned in.

Ryton took a lapis lazuli stone from the hidden compartment and held it up. "It's some sort of charm, I think."

The stone held a carving of an oak leaf on a sun. "More oaks." Vahly rolled her eyes and shared a grin with Nix.

But it was time now to stop stalling and mooning. Vahly marched to the walls and began searching for birthplace markers.

Arc disappeared into one of the lesser chambers but appeared again quickly. "No markers in that room."

Vahly found nothing on the first wall, so she headed into the next chamber with Arc. Nix and Ryton searched the far wall, unspeaking but not fighting either, which seemed like a good sign for this temporary and bizarre band they'd created.

The second chamber was empty. The third as well.

The group left the house and began searching the next. And the next.

Ryton's face had grown ashen. He wasn't going to be able to hold off the water much longer. Everyone was quiet, and the silence, touched only by the sea's hissing against Ryton's spell, unsettled Vahly and made her jumpy.

The sixth structure they came to was narrower than the others, with a peaked stone entrance that remained whole. The roof was gone, of course; Vahly was fairly certain these homes had used thatch roofing. Kyril lifted into the air and flew above the group as they began to search the building's snaking corridors and chambers. Vahly stepped over a pile of wine amphoras, crockery that must have held such things as honey or goat's milk, and stacks of cracked plates and mugs.

Ryton walked behind her, Nix close enough to burn him alive if he did something they didn't like.

Vahly's magic punched against her heart, and she stopped, putting a hand over her chest.

"It's here. Somewhere," she whispered.

Kyril landed between Ryton and Vahly, tucking his wings tightly to fit into the round room.

The curved walls showed five dark red stone tablets. The names on the first four blurred as tears pricked Vahly's eyes. This was her family's home. She knew it. The truth of it pumped through her veins. And these tablets showed her parents' names and those of her two siblings.

She had a brother and a sister.

"Antton," Ryton said, reading the birth marker for

Vahly's brother. "I believe it means One Who Is Beyond Price."

Vahly swallowed. What had this older brother looked like? Had he cared for Vahly when she was an infant? She kissed her fingers and touched the stone before moving to her sister's tablet again.

"And this one?" she asked Ryton. She could barely speak for the emotions surging through her and the magic thundering through her blood.

Ryton cocked his head and squinted, the circles under his eyes darkening with every minute he held the spell. "Irati. Her name means something along the lines of plants, but I can't be certain."

She was named for something of the earth. A smile pulled at Vahly's mouth. She kissed the stone and stepped over to her own birth marker.

"Vahly," Ryton said quietly. "Blooded for the battle." He faced her, a confusion of feelings swirling in his eyes. "Your dragons killed my sister. But my kynd killed your family. We must end this, Earth Queen. Will you balance the world instead of seeking to slay all of the sea folk? Will you be the queen I wish Astraea was?"

Vahly soaked in the presence of Kyril, Arc, and Nix, drawing strength from them. "I will do my best, General, but I'd be lying if I said this was a sure bet."

Nix chuckled. "Such a Vahly thing to say. She's nothing if not genuine."

Ryton bent his head briefly, then met Vahly's eyes. "Then carry on. I will do my part."

Now what? Vahly pet Kyril's head, his feathers soft under her calloused hands.

Kyril flashed an image of Vahly's face. She almost appeared to be glowing.

Nerves sparking, Vahly closed her eyes and focused on the magic flowing through her veins. She stepped forward, keeping a hand on Kyril as she stood directly in front of the stone marker.

A buzzing traveled from the soles of her bare feet, up her legs, into her torso, and all the way to the crown of her head. She felt taller, stronger…more.

Words threaded into her mind, and her lips opened to speak them.

CHAPTER THIRTY-THREE

"I am Vahly, Blooded for the Battle, and I have found my familiar, Kyril of the Western Gryphons. I claim my birthright to rise up as Earth Queen and create balance in this world."

The ground trembled. Sand fell from the cracks between the stones. Kyril tossed his head, and Vahly held tightly to his pelt, fingers digging into his warm fur.

The scent of rain, roots, turned earth, and crushed leaves filled the air as a warmth like sunlight rushed down Vahly's body.

She opened her eyes, feeling like a new creature. "Rise," she commanded the earth.

The ground she stood on lifted both her and Kyril but did not disturb the birthplaces of Vahly's family. Arc, Nix, and Ryton stared as the earth multiplied itself and became a small peak that looked out at the Lost Valley, the Lapis palace, and the ocean.

And Vahly felt no fatigue from the magic. None. This power was a part of her now, not something she had to stretch and reach for. Raising this peak had been like making a fist. Simple.

Kyril spread his wings and crowed triumphantly as Vahly peered down at Arc, Nix, and Ryton. Arc spun his air magic, wind coursing through his hair and whipping his clothes about, and he jumped impossibly high to join them atop the peak. Nix flew up and gathered Vahly into a hug.

"I knew you could do this, Vahl," she whispered, her words bursting with hope that Vahly prayed she wouldn't have to disappoint.

"Earth Queen!" Ryton shouted from below. "Astraea—"

His spell failed. Water crashed back into place.

Nix sucked a breath, fearing the spelled salt water despite Arc's magic.

Ryton's body twisted in the sudden wave, but he fought the current and returned, his head breaking through the foaming sea and his hair black against his head. "Astraea comes!"

Heart thrashing, Vahly climbed atop Kyril and held a hand out for Arc. He took it and sat behind her. Nix flew toward the coastline, her movements erratic as Kyril trailed after.

Vahly twisted to see Ryton in the water, but his focus was on whatever was happening beyond the Lost Valley.

She began to shout a question, but the water shivered violently as it drew away from the shore.

Vahly went cold all over.

Kyril whirled, and the ocean came fully into view.

Arc clutched Vahly tightly and whispered sharply in elvish. "Vahly, love, what can I do?"

He sounded as lost as she felt. Until they saw what Astraea was doing, there was little to do but watch.

A tremor passed over the sea's surface.

A wave clawed its way out of the depths—a mountain of gray and foaming water—and headed directly for the Lapis palace.

"No!" Vahly gripped Kyril's body with her legs. "Go, Kyril!"

Kyril shot through the air, passing over the Lost Valley as the wave careened into the flooded civilization and smashed onto shore. Salt water splashed high, stinging Vahly's cheeks and eyes. Kyril's wingtips flared as he dodged a fist of spelled water, but then another crest of water leapt and yanked them out of the sky.

Water cold as death broke Vahly's hold on Kyril and she tumbled head over feet as the ocean raked salty fingers over her skin and through her hair. The undertow spun her around and dragged her deeper.

It was like Astraea herself was pulling her into a watery grave.

Arc was nowhere to be seen. Kyril, Ryton, Nix. All gone.

Salt water burned Vahly's nostrils and throat. Shaking with the need to breathe, lungs on fire, she focused on her power and summoned the earth to save her. Her stomach dropped as a spit of land suddenly rose from the seabed and lifted her above the punching waves. The land was listening even now, even as the ocean smothered it with skillful, murderous hands.

Shaking, Vahly scrambled to her feet, and the earth beneath her steadied. Frantic, wild, she searched the water for Kyril and Arc.

And then she turned to see the Lapis palace, her second home, safe place for her beloved new family.

The sea wrapped the mountains in dark arms, waves licking up the sides, toward the very top of the main section of the palace.

Dragons flew around the peak, slashes of sapphire in the bone-white sky, dashing in to lift the injured. Those unable to fly crowded in their shadows, wings spread, screaming for help, blasting dragonfire as their bodies burned under the black touch of the spelled salt water.

Vahly realized she was screaming too.

She felt as if her head would burst.

Waves rocked the mountain, breaking off massive chunks of the palace. In the white ash currents swarming the peaks, bodies rose to the surface, eyes open, wings and scales black.

"Did you believe you would escape?" Astraea rose on the crest of a knife-sharp wave, her scarlet coral spear lifted and her face glowing with triumph. "Did you think you could best me?"

Vahly spat salt from her mouth. Kyril broke through the surface and extended a wing. Vahly's heart squeezed, her magic drumming impossibly fast inside her chest as Kyril screeched and she summoned the land to lift him from the water. He floundered on the rising mound of sandy ground.

"No!" Astraea shouted. "You do not get to escape. You have lost, Earth Queen!" She pointed her spear at Kyril, and a curl of ocean hammered Kyril's new island and threw him into the water again. The fins of sea creatures raced from Astraea toward Kyril.

There was a shout. Ryton was lifting Arc from the water, helping Nix, who'd changed into full dragon form, pull him from the chaos of eddies. When Nix had Arc, Ryton leapt from the water toward Kyril. In the air, he shouted to Astraea.

"Your rule is over, murderer. For Grystark!"

He dove under, then reemerged, his spear held aloft, his spellwork pulling Kyril from the sea on a shelf of bubbling water. As Astraea aimed another massive wave at Kyril, the gryphon took to the sky, shaking his wings and aiming for Vahly, who couldn't breathe because her heart was breaking.

Ryton leapt from the waves. "Win this for us, Earth Queen!"

He drove his spelled wave at Astraea to distract her. She whirled to face him, then directed all her power—twisting currents and leaping sea beasts—at her former lover, her general. Ryton went down. Blood filled Vahly's vision, swirls of dark red blackening the water.

Kyril swooped low, and Vahly jumped onto his back, salty wind whipping her face and drawing the tears from her eyes.

They raced toward the Lapis, Arc and Nix flying beside them.

A crowd of Call Breakers—Aitor, Euskal, and Baww among them—flew from the direction of the Dragon's Back, heading for the Lapis palace, ready to help.

Amona stood atop the mountain. Helena, Ruda, and about two dozen more Lapis gathered around her. They were helping dragons out of the oculus that crowned the main section of the palace.

"Fly, my dragons!" Amona's eyes were wild as she gestured, urging them on.

With faces drawn and fear stunting their normally graceful movements, those dragons who had been trained as warriors and who were used to the threat of spelled salt water took off, flying over the submersed Red Meadow, toward the northern mountains where they might find dry land.

Some Call Breakers joined them, while others grabbed the frightened dragons and pulled them into the sky, forcing them to fly despite their terror.

Rigel, Ursae, and Haldus climbed from the oculus and reached for Euskal, who hovered at the peak so they could leap onto his back.

"Mother!" Vahly shouted as they came close. "Get out of there, Mother! Please!"

"Take them, Vahly! Take them north! I will go when all are safe!"

"To Ruda," Vahly said to Kyril.

He veered around the peak and took the back of Ruda's dress between his teeth.

Vahly held a hand down to Ruda as they circled back around. She was too frightened to fly over the spelled salt water, the poor thing. "Grab my hand, Ruda. It's all right. We'll go back for more of our own."

Ruda's cold fingers gripped Vahly's sweaty hand, and soon enough Ruda was riding behind her. Kyril grabbed another dragon. It was Helena. Vahly helped Helena half fly, half climb up Kyril's body until the healer was seated behind Ruda.

Arc and Nix pulled two younglings up with them. Then

they saved a one-winged dragon, injured in a long-ago battle and who had worked in the kitchens.

Kyril was struggling, panting, weakened by the wave that had struck him. He couldn't carry any more. Vahly asked him to circle the peak.

She focused on the drumming in her veins and envisioned the land beneath the water, near the bridge where her kynd had once worked side by side. She imagined the red hat flowers that bloomed there, the scent of the grasses, the heat on the dirt path.

"Arc! Nix! Can you combine your magic with mine?" Vahly shouted over the endless crash of more and more waves and Astraea's far-off cackling. Gripping Kyril's ruff, she commanded the earth. "Rise. Rise for my dragons."

Her body began to shake, and Ruda held her tightly, little talons cutting into Vahly's stomach. Arc wove sparkling gold and purple threads and expanded the colors and light toward the space in front of Vahly and Kyril's flight direction. Nix blew dragonfire toward Kyril, who held his path, wings steady and a growl growing in his chest, vibrating through Vahly's bones like an elixir for strength.

Vahly used her power to push the varying magicks in the same direction.

In the spot where Vahly imagined the bridge used to stand, a blast of green fire and blinding light hit the water. The salt water twisted into a plume of white steam that soared into the western sky. The bridge was there, and the land on either side of it shuddered, cracked, then lifted into the air, becoming two peaks, dry as high summer.

The dragons who were not warriors took the chance and

flew from the top of the mountain palace to Vahly's new peaks, farther from the riotous ocean and Astraea's control.

Astraea's thundering commands faded, and the sea calmed, leaving the palace and the majority of the Red Meadow underwater.

Vahly and Kyril followed Arc and Nix. They landed on the first of the two new peaks and the dragons gathered.

"We will find a place in the North to shelter." The desire to kill Astraea burned like a brand on Vahly's heart, but the dragons came first. "Come. We must go now."

As they flew off to find this promised safe place, Vahly turned to check on Amona. She stood still, eyes unblinking, with bodies of dying dragons at her feet.

Come with us, Mother. There is nothing more you can do.

I am defeated, Daughter. The Lapis are dead. Our home is a tomb.

We are not beaten. Some of us live still, and we will fight!

Even with her newfound strength, gained at her birthplace, Vahly felt like she didn't stand a chance against the Sea Queen. Astraea was so quick to strike and seemed to know where and when to hit to make the most damage.

Vahly couldn't grasp the enormity of the task that fate had set at her feet. How could she plan this defeat of Astraea? How could she balance the world? Such an intangible goal.

But she wouldn't give up.

In fact, she relished a long shot bet.

The fight against Astraea would come, and Vahly would gladly spill her own blood or Astraea's to win it. She only hoped there would be someone left to save.

Her magic jerked her ribs and flared hot in her heart. A

realization swept over her. She had to visit the Sacred Oak, the one her kynd had spoken of in the scrolls she'd read in the Lapis library.

I have one more step to take. If I visit the Sacred Oak, my power will rise in full. I will be Astraea's downfall, I swear this to you, my mother and my matriarch. I refuse to fail you.

CHAPTER THIRTY-FOUR

Ryton shut his eyes as he sank below the cresting waves, the sound of water magic shushing in his ears. The sea swaddled him in smooth and gentle hands, and he opened his eyes to see nothing but a broad expanse of shimmering blue. No dragons. No Astraea. No blood.

His body felt strange. Light. He crossed his arms over his chest, slipping into the feel of the current running through his hair and over his skin.

A sudden thought occurred to him, and he touched his shoulder.

The black beast was gone.

How? What had happened after he'd battled Astraea to save the Earth Queen's familiar?

A voice threaded through the sound of magic. "Brother, you are a hero."

A sob choked Ryton's answer.

"Be well. It is over." Selene's slender face appeared before him.

She tilted her head, and strands of her braided hair came loose around her proud cheeks and chin. Her fingers traced the scars on his face, her touch wiping them away like the marks were an artist's mistake.

"How?" he asked.

"Your soul drew me here."

"You're not angry with me for helping them?" Ryton's voice cracked. "I thought you might understand. She is so much like you."

Selene's smile was sunshine illuminating the curve of a shore-bound wave. "Of course not. It's what I would have done. You did it for me. For all of us."

A host of sea folk swam into view behind Selene, faces peaceful and full of joy.

"We don't need to dominate," a deep voice said.

Ryton turned to see who it was, to see if his shaking heart could be right.

Grystark nodded and touched Ryton's shoulder. "We need to balance."

"But Lilia—"

"She is strong. She fights for this balance, and she won't fault you for your actions. I have visited her. She taught me the purpose of a rebellion."

The coolness of deep water eased the last of his pains as all but Selene faded from view. Ryton breathed deep, gills flaring and his fins rippling along his arms and legs. Selene swam alongside him. She put her hand in his like they'd done when they were young, and they headed into the great open ocean.

At last, Ryton was not a lover, a general, or a tortured assassin.

Finally, he was free.

CHAPTER THIRTY-FIVE

Great pools of salt water lay around the northern mountains like the land itself had bled out in murky shades of gray and blue. Kyril pumped his wings, then soared down to a treeless flat on the top of one of the highest points.

They'd flown the full distance in silence, none calling out or speaking telepathically. It was as if the quiet, the sound of wind and wings only, had served to steel them up for what would come next and what they would have to face upon landing. They'd lost so many. And there would be ongoing questions about survivors yet undiscovered. There were the Jades to think of too. A messenger would need to be sent.

Nix alighted beside Kyril and Vahly, and everyone else —Helena, Ruda, Lapis younglings, the one-winged kitchen Lapis, numerous Call Breakers, and around thirty adult Lapis—gathered around Vahly.

Magic knocked a steady rhythm against her heart as she thought of Amona. Had she taken off? Was she alive? Was she headed here now, or was she still trying to save more Lapis from high places they had missed in their desperate flight to escape?

Kyril flashed an image into Vahly's mind. An oak with gnarled limbs spread roots under a carpet of bright yellow eguzkilore with prickly, sage-green leaves. The expanse of thistle flowers made it seem as if the sun itself had broken into a thousand pieces and fallen to the oak's feet. This was the Sacred Oak. Immediately, Vahly thought of the Forest of Illumahrah, and, of course, the disaster that had destroyed it.

"Where did you see the Sacred Oak?" she asked Kyril aloud.

"What is it?" Arc finished healing the injured, his crown of day and night swirling around his head and his fingers limned in sparkling magic.

"I must go to the Sacred Oak. Kyril has seen it. But I thought it was in the Forest of Illumahrah. I feel like it's there. But how can it be there still after all that happened?"

Kyril showed Vahly an adult male and female gryphon. They flicked their tails in the same way Kyril often did. The oak materialized between them.

Vahly looked at Arc. "Is there something such as hereditary memory? Because I'm fairly certain Kyril just showed me that he has some of his parents' memories."

"I don't know the magic of the gryphons. I'd say it's possible. As for where the Sacred Oak is, I don't know. If we go back to Illumahrah..." His voice broke, and he glanced at Rigel, Haldus, and Ursae. "We might find it is submerged again."

Vahly's magic pushed, insistent, demanding that she

leave now for the elves' demolished homeland. "I have to try."

Helena was crying quietly. "But Vahly, if you get there and there is no place to land, you'll die."

"I can raise the land we need." At least she hoped she would be able to. If Astraea attacked at the wrong moment, she might not have the time. "Who will go with me?"

In full dragon form, Amona soared out of the sky, her sapphire wings turning the sun into shadow. She held two injured Lapis in her foreclaws. Three more rode atop her back.

I will come with you, Daughter, Amona said inside Vahly's mind.

Helena, Ruda, and Arc rushed over to help the wounded.

"Matriarch Amona will fly with me," Vahly said, forcing the torn pieces of her soul to stay together. "Who else is with me?"

Arc finished healing the Lapis, then stood, his face solemn and his cloak whipping in the wind. "Do you even need to ask?" He smiled grimly.

His words sealed a portion of her soul back together. "Thank you, King Arcturus."

Nix, in her human form, crossed her arms. "You're always going to be stuck with me, Queenie."

Vahly put a hand on Nix's shoulder, and they traded a look that held more shared emotions than Vahly could voice aloud.

Aitor was whispering with Baww and Euskal. Euskal's face was blank with shock. Aitor spun to face Vahly and Nix. "If it's all right with Nix, I'm game for the adventure."

"You're well enough now?" Nix asked eyeing his scales to check for plague symptoms, but he looked hearty and hale to Vahly.

"As healthy as any of us can be, I'd imagine." Aitor's gaze flicked to Amona, who remained in her full dragon form, staring past the mountaintops in the direction of her palace.

Vahly longed for a moment of comfort. Her arms ached to hold Arc. He seemed to sense her longing and hurried to her side. She pulled him away from the group.

"Arc…" A shudder shook her as she tried to get the words out. "The Lapis… I thought Astraea had taken you under for good. I thought we were all dead."

Arc took her face in his hands, and a tingling warmth sparked her cheeks where his fingertips touched skin. Concern filled his eyes. "My queen. You saved us. And you will again."

She brushed a hand over his chest, her thumb catching on his sharp collarbone and the muscle underneath his cloak. "We combined our magic. It worked. But still, she was so fast."

There was no need to say who she was talking about. She knew well he was imagining the horror of Queen Astraea's cresting, impossible wave just as clearly as her.

Arc drew her close, and she pressed her nose beneath his chin, smelling the pine sap and mint scent of his air magic. His presence was another cloak on her shoulders, luxurious, velvet, warm. But they had to keep moving. There was no time to dwell on these pleasures. Astraea would come again, and she would finish them next time.

Vahly broke away from Arc slowly, reluctantly, then led

him to the edge of the drop where Aitor and Nix stood talking in hushed whispers.

Wind sheared up the cliff and snaked into collars and around throats, a cold like death in its touch. Kyril and Amona spread their wings behind the smaller group, holding off some of the northern air, protecting with sinew, flesh, bone, and feather.

Vahly brushed her arm against Arc's body to feel his warmth and soak in his presence. Then she took Nix's hand, memorizing the feel of every scale and the impressions of treasured rings—destroyed when Nix had suddenly shifted form during the attack—now lost along with life as they had known it, their homes, and so many loved ones.

The sunset poured fire across the endless blade of sea that had brought the island to its knees.

"Thank you, Ryton. I hope you found peace." Vahly's voice was as rough as the rocky soil beneath her feet. She glanced at Amona, Kyril, Arc, Nix, and Aitor, taking strength from the fight in their eyes.

"Even if we fail," she said, raising her raw voice to battle the sound of wind and water, "I'm proud to have fought beside you, to have called you friends."

Pre-order the next book, SWORD OF OAK, today! http:// hyperurl.co/SwordofOakqos

For FREE reads from Alisha, including a BONUS SCENE from

the first book in this series, head to https://www.alishaklapheke.
com/free-prequel-1

OTHER BOOKS BY ALISHA KLAPHEKE

The Edinburgh Seer Trilogy
The Uncommon World Series
Rune Kingdom (An Uncommon World standalone novel)
Once Upon An Enchanted Forest (THE MATCHWEAVER'S
LOOM—will become a series in mid 2020)

Books under Alisha's paranormal romance pen name, Eve
A. Hunt
Fae Curse (January 2020)
Fae World (February 2020)
Fae Spell (March 2020)
If you want to receive updates on Eve's books and free scenes, go
to https://www.alishaklapheke.com/eve-a-hunt

And now for a sneak peek of Alisha's EDINBURGH SEER, a
fantasy set in an magical, alternate Edinburgh where the British
Empire still reigns supreme and technology is a bit different than
what we're used to...

THE EDINBURGH SEER

BOOK ONE SNEAK PEEK

Summer, 2017, Fifteenth Year of John III's Reign

The morning sun had just managed to paint a pale yellow light over Edinburgh's Old Town, and, as usual, Aini MacGregor had already run three errands and set up her father's candy lab for the day's work. Pots, scrubbed and warmed, on the stove. Measuring spoons shined to make the morning sun jealous. Bags of powdered sugar and vials of hormones and chemicals standing in place like disciplined kingsmen. Everything was exactly where it needed to be.

The tower was chilly this time of day and goosebumps hurried over Aini's skin as she unscrewed a jar and shifted the newly purchased cinnamon into its tidy home. She inhaled the lovely scent. Tears burned her eyes—not because of the many spices she had at her fingertips, but because of the rasping voice carried on the wind through the cracked, leaded window above her head—the voice of

Nathair Campbell, the very powerful man who would shoot her dead if he knew what she was.

A sixth-senser.

Demanding her skittering heart to quit distracting her, Aini continued about her work. Today would be a great one for her father, Lewis MacGregor, crafter of the nobility's beloved sweets. Together, with the apprentices' help, they shaped goodies that not only tasted divine, but gave the eater certain short-term abilities usually enjoyed by birds or insects, or only dreamed up by wild imaginations. They'd been a hit at the king's last birthday party. The British king was a terrible man—Aini couldn't change that—but at least his parties helped with business. With the vision-inducing gum they were about to craft and test, the MacGregor business, Enliven, was poised to rule the boutique sweets market. If only the stupid thugs, the Campbells, would leave well enough alone.

Clan Campbell worked for the king, maintaining his rules here in Scotland. But lately...they seemed to have become very full of themselves and were taking on projects that Aini was certain the king himself knew nothing about.

"Who is shouting to wake the dead in the Grassmarket?" Neve demanded in place of a *Good Morning*. Father's female apprentice padded into the room. When she wasn't working in the lab, Neve took tourists around Scotland with Caledonia Tours. She knew her history, that was for sure.

With quick fingers and a smile, the Edinburgh native pulled her hair into two high buns and secured them with pins. All the girls here wore their hair like that. Aini tugged at one of her own heavy, black locks. It refused to be tied up, but even though it made her stand out—not many half Balinese girls in Scotland—she couldn't hate it. It reminded her of her mom, a woman who hadn't been perfect, but who'd loved her completely.

Aini straightened her lab coat and eyed the king's rules hanging on the wall. An identical list of "Scottish citizens cannot do this" and "All citizens and colonials must do that" were posted in every pub, home, and store in the entire British Empire. Even across the pond in the rebellious Dominion of New England colonies. Aini wondered if they'd ever get over their 18th century loss. They were nearly as bad as the Scottish rebels here.

Blinking, she remembered Neve's earlier question. "Nathair Campbell is down there, dirtying the morning."

Neve made a Scottish sound of disgust in the back of her throat. Aini couldn't have agreed more. "I'm excited about that new gum recipe," Neve said.

Perfectly on time—because Aini perfectly timed it—the gum base started to bubble on the stove.

"Your white pepper idea for the gum is going to work. I can feel it." Aini wiped her hands on a towel, breathing in the sweet smells. "I really think it'll trigger the chewer's schema for fire."

Neve grinned, and Aini realized her Dominion of New England accent was blazing again.

Thane loped into the lab, and Aini's heart whirred like a broken taffy puller and pushed every other thought out of her head. At six-foot-four, the Scotsman dominated the room, all broad shoulders, gray flashing eyes, and downturned mouth. He pulled his glasses out of his messy, honey-colored hair and headed toward his lab coat on the far hook. Mud caked the toes of his boots, and a silver necklace winked from his collarbone.

Because of who Aini was, and *what* Aini was, Thane with his late nights and penchant for whisky was the very definition of *Look, but don't touch*. She had to be careful. Do nothing dangerous. Never break any rules.

"Good morning, Thane."

Just because he wasn't for her didn't mean she had to be rude. After all, he was Father's favorite, besides herself, of course. Thane had developed the original formula for the vision gum. Aini wished she had half the brains he did.

"We're almost ready to mix," she said.

His gaze slid over her fingers and up her arms, and he gave her a nod.

As Neve measured out the pepper, Aini held a hand toward the bubbling broiler. "A little help?" she asked Thane. Her face heated. Why did her cheeks have to flush so easily?

"Aye. Course." Thane's thick, West Scots accent wrapped around every O and tripped over each R beautifully.

Tugging his coat on, Thane slid his glasses onto his slightly overlarge nose. Tattoos of chemical formulas snaked down his fingers in black letters, tiny numbers, and mathematical symbols. Aini leaned forward a little. NaCl was salt. Another finger had a *V* over a *t* and—*oh*—it was the formula for viscosity. But the other markings? She could never quite get a good look at them.

Father walked in, wearing his usual style—all black under his lab coat, and every item ironed into full submission. He winked before readying the powdered sugar at the lab's silver table. He still wore his wedding ring, though the divorce happened long before Aini's mother died two years ago. She sighed, wishing she could do something about that pain.

"I was thinking," Father said to Thane, "if we used a pressure cooker to force the Maillard reaction in tomorrow's Dulce de Leche recipe…"

Thane's face brightened. "We could decrease the cooking time by perhaps six times." Thane lifted the pot as Aini stirred. His arm brushed hers and she swallowed. "Genius, Mr. MacGregor," Thane said.

"Will you never stop with the Mr. MacGregor? Just Lewis, please."

Thane smiled at Father like he was his own, like Father could somehow heal the hurt that clouded the uni student's eyes. But it was all right. She wasn't jealous. Aini knew Father was good at providing a stable life, a simple and scheduled way of living, something maybe Thane hadn't experienced before apprenticing here.

"Neve, will you please warm up the mixer?" Father wiped a spot of sugar off his nose and set his planner on the desk near the far end of the lab. The green and blue sugar, in the jars he'd mounted on the whitewashed wall, sparkled. He frowned like there was something unpleasant about them. Aini touched her chin. She'd always wondered why he displayed the jars like that. They'd never used those colored sugars and surely it would be better to have them with the other ingredients, organized by the lab table. She'd look into it later.

Father shook his head and went to help Thane pour the steaming gum base into the powdered sugar.

The lab's landline rang and Aini picked up. A familiar, rough voice asked for Lewis MacGregor. Aini gritted her teeth. Not *them* again. Her grip on the phone tightened.

"Hold please." She looked to Father. "It's for you."

He stared at the ceiling, eyes pressed closed, before finally taking the call.

While Neve dealt with the mixer's perpetually moody switch across the room—all while humming a song loved by Father's other male apprentice, Myles—Aini took Father's place beside Thane.

Plunging her hands into the gum blend, she kneaded the sticky stuff. The mix was ready for flavor. The powdered sage, white pepper, and smoky nutmeg did nothing to improve the color of the chewing gum, but she was pretty sure Neve was on to something with this flavor choice. The herbs and spices, along with the medieval art packaging that Myles had drawn up, might just get people seeing ancient castles and feasts in great halls. Chemistry crossed with suggestion. It was how the human brain worked.

"No." Father's knuckles whitened as he squeezed the phone. "I'm not going to weaponize my products. Not until I see the royal approval. I'm finished talking about this." He punched a button and threw the phone to his desk where it banged against his laptop. "Campbells. Pushing and pushing. Playing both sides, and I know very well I'm not going to be the winner no matter how…" Muttering, he stalked back to the table. "I need to get something from my downstairs office. Give me a shout when we're ready to test." He disappeared down the staircase, growling about being left in peace.

The Campbells made up the majority of kingsmen stationed in Edinburgh. Normally, they were the law, acting as the king's agents, along with the other kingsmen. But since that public execution of those rebels last month, things had been different. Nathair Campbell had executed Scottish subjects without a trial of any kind. The king had excused him, blaming overzealous loyalty to the crown, but Aini wasn't so sure. Clan Campbell was less an arm of the king and more of a criminal gang these days. Aini couldn't believe they were pressuring Father to develop products that could covertly paralyze and poison without the king's seal of approval. Even if it was to fight the rebels. It was unfathomable.

Thane breathed hard through his nose like an angry horse.

She eyed the gum, looking for dry spots or uneven spicing. "What is it? What's off?"

Vine-like muscles twisted below Thane's rolled coat sleeves. He dusted his hands off and pushed his glasses into his hair. "If your father would agree to aid the Campbells, he'd be helping Scotland fight the rebels."

"He doesn't want to twist our craft into something sick and evil." She put her hands on her hips and powdered sugar puffed like little clouds. Flushing, she brushed herself off. "He's worked long and hard to establish Enliven. It's a boutique candy supplier. Not a government laboratory. Besides that, why can't the Campbells go through the official channels and find their own chemists if they're so set on this?"

Neve gathered the pre-blended gum mix. "Because Mr.

MacGregor is the best chemist in the empire and they know it."

"Well, we're going to follow the official rules." Aini crossed her arms. "The king could shut us down and you know it."

Neve opened her mouth and closed it again. She hurried to the mixer and dropped her bundle into the metal bowl.

Aini chewed the inside of her cheek. She didn't want to be hard on Neve, but the rules were the rules.

"The Campbells and the king have the same goal, don't they?" Thane frowned. "What difference does fussing about with royal seals make?"

"If my father skirts the law like the Campbells want him to do, the Campbells might get away with it, but I seriously doubt he will."

An image flashed through her memory—an executed sixth-senser.

The woman had been about her mother's age. Aini remembered the lady's wispy, auburn hair. The black band across her eyes. Her body jerking as the bullet hit her chest. The red blood against her striped dress. Her clothing said native Edinburgh, the style Aini tried to imitate. But even fitting in hadn't saved her.

If Aini was found out, the Campbells would assume Father knew about her ability, which he didn't. She squeezed her hands together. She couldn't even think about him rotting in a dark cell.

When the gum was mixed and cooled, Thane cut the ropes into small pieces and Aini called her father back up to the lab. It was time to see if the gum really worked.

The light through the lab's windows cast a net of gold around Aini's father as he peered at his watch. He handed Aini the clipboard of notes they'd destroy as soon as the trial was complete. They couldn't let anyone outside of Enliven get a hold of the information. The competition would leap at the chance to outdo them. Because of this, Aini and the rest had become very, very good at remembering recipes.

Neve and Aini found seats and Thane took a stool, ready to try the gum.

"Where is Myles anyway?" Neve asked.

Aini was actually glad Father's second male apprentice wasn't here. "Buying new paints for his adverts." Myles was great fun, but he could really be a distraction during tests like this.

Father stared at Thane. "I want to know the very minute —the exact moment—you see something." He started the timer on his watch.

"Aye," Thane popped the gum between his lips and chewed, rubbing a hand over his sharp chin.

"How's it taste, then?" Neve scooted forward on her stool.

"A bit fiery."

"Fiery?" Aini asked, pen poised over the clipboard. "Be more specific. We need details for the investors."

"Any visions yet?" Father inched closer to Thane.

Stumbling back, Thane's mouth dropped open, the gum on his tongue.

Aini laughed.

Father practically hopped on Thane. "What do you see, lad?" He normally hid his accent, wanting to please his many English clients, but excitement drew it right out of him.

Staring at the ceiling beams, Thane paled. "Translucent wings. About ten feet long. He's...he's..." The uni student ducked and laughed once, his Adam's apple bobbing in his throat. "He's breathing fire." He shoved his hands through his hair and knocked his glasses to the floor.

Neve hugged herself. "A dragon."

Father lifted his feet in a little jig and grabbed Aini's arm, pulling her into his dance. Heart light, she did a spin, then squeezed him, feeling safe and loved, as if everything was going to be okay.

"I can't believe it," Thane whispered.

Neve grinned. "I knew that white pepper would do the trick."

"Couldn't have done it without you, my wee squirrel," Father said to Aini. "The king will reward us handsomely, what with his birthday celebration coming up. We might get a tax exemption."

"And the elite will want it at their parties if the king has it at his," she said.

Father shouted, "Huzzah!" and zipped over to his desk to write something up.

Aini couldn't stop smiling. Another candy for their impressive inventory. Another building block for Father's beloved business. Somehow, she had to thank the apprentices for all their hard work. Maybe a special dinner or a big night out. This vision-inducing gum was another reason she loved having all of them here, a part of the family.

Neve peppered Thane with questions about the

formula. Over Neve's head, Thane met Aini's gaze. A shadow passed over his face. He was a melancholy sort, but this was more. Something…darker. Aini's smile faded. He had nothing to be upset about today. What could be bothering him? Surely not all this stuff about the Campbells. It would pass. Wouldn't it?

Father tugged Aini into another jubilant hug, and her smile returned. She could maintain this happiness. She would maintain it. No matter what. She just had to keep her sixth sense concealed. Because visions prompted by chewing gum earned money, but visions of another sort only led to death.

Read the rest of THE EDINBURGH SEER today!

https://www.amazon.com/dp/B07BP1ZNPR

www.ingramcontent.com/pod-product-compliance
Lightning Source LLC
Chambersburg PA
CBHW021656110726
47902CB00007B/1953